Three Bedrooms in Manhattan

'I love reading Simenon. He makes me t

'A truly wonderful writer . . . marvellou
simple, absolutely in tune with the world he creates'

— Muriel Spark

'Few writers have ever conveyed with such a sure touch,
the bleakness of human life'

— A. N. Wilson

'One of the greatest writers of the twentieth century . . . Simenon
was unequalled at making us look inside, though the ability was
masked by his brilliance at absorbing us obsessively in his stories'

— *Guardian*

'A novelist who entered his fictional world as if he were part of it'

— Peter Ackroyd

'The greatest of all, the most genuine novelist we have had in literature'

— André Gide

'Superb . . . The most addictive of writers . . . A unique teller of tales'

— *Observer*

'The mysteries of the human personality are revealed in all their
disconcerting complexity'

— Anita Brookner

'A writer who, more than any other crime novelist, combined a high
literary reputation with popular appeal'

— P. D. James

'A supreme writer . . . Unforgettable vividness'

— *Independent*

'Compelling, remorseless, brilliant'

— John Gray

'Extraordinary masterpieces of the twentieth century'

— John Banville

Georges Simenon was born in Liège, Belgium, in 1903. He is best known in Britain as the author of the Maigret novels and his prolific output of over 400 novels and short stories have made him a household name in continental Europe. He died in 1989 in Lausanne, Switzerland, where he had lived for the latter part of his life.

GEORGES SIMENON

Three Bedrooms in Manhattan

Translated by MARC ROMANO
AND LAWRENCE G. BLOCHMAN

PENGUIN BOOKS

PENGUIN CLASSICS

UK | USA | Canada | Ireland | Australia
India | New Zealand | South Africa

Penguin Books is part of the Penguin Random House group of companies whose
addresses can be found at global.penguinrandomhouse.com.

Penguin
Random House
UK

First published in French as *Trois Chambres à Manhattan* 1946
This translation first published by the *New York Review of Books* 2003
Published in Penguin Classics 2020
001

Set in 12.5/15 pt Dante MT Std by Integra Software Services Pvt. Ltd, Pondicherry
Printed and bound in Great Britain by Clays Ltd, Elcograf S.p.A.

A CIP catalogue record for this book is available
from the British Library

ISBN: 978-0-241-46156-3

www.greenpenguin.co.uk

MIX
Paper from
responsible sources
FSC® C018179

Penguin Random House is committed to a
sustainable future for our business, our readers
and our planet. This book is made from Forest
Stewardship Council® certified paper.

Three Bedrooms in Manhattan

He woke up suddenly at 3.00 a.m., dead tired, got dressed, and almost went out without his tie, in slippers, coat collar turned up, like people who walk their dogs late at night or very early in the morning. Then, when he was in the courtyard of the building, where after two months he still couldn't bring himself to feel at home, he glanced upward mechanically and realized that he'd forgotten to turn out his light, but he didn't have the energy to climb back up the stairs.

What were they doing, up there in J.K.C.'s apartment? Was Winnie vomiting yet? Probably. Moaning, at first softly, then more loudly, until at last she burst into an endless fit of tears.

His footsteps resounded in the nearly empty streets of Greenwich Village, and he was still thinking about the couple who once more had made it impossible for him to sleep. He had never seen them. He didn't even know what the initials J.K.C. stood for. He'd read them, painted in green, on his neighbor's door.

And he knew, after passing by one morning when the door was open, that the floor was black, probably varnished – a glistening black lacquer that was all the more striking in contrast to the red furniture inside.

He knew a lot about the two of them, but only in pieces he couldn't quite fit together. That J.K.C. was a painter. That Winnie lived in Boston.

What did she do? Why did she always come to New York on Friday nights, and only on Friday nights? Why didn't she ever stay the whole weekend? Well, of course there were jobs where people had different days off. She came by taxi, probably from the train station, just before eight. Always the same time, give or take a few minutes – that's what made him think she'd arrived by train.

At first her voice would be shrill and piercing. She had two voices. He could hear her, bustling about, speaking with the animation of someone who was just stopping by.

They ate dinner in the studio. Like clockwork the meal was delivered from an Italian restaurant in the neighborhood fifteen minutes before she arrived.

J.K.C. spoke little, his voice muffled. Despite the thinness of the walls, it was impossible to make out what he was saying, apart from a word or two on those nights when he called Boston.

And why did he never call before midnight, and often not until long after one?

'Hello . . . long distance?'

Then Combe knew that it would go on for hours. 'Boston' he could recognize but not the name of the exchange. Then the name 'Winnie' and a surname starting with a *p*, an *o*, an *l*. He never caught the last few letters.

Then the endless hushed whispering.

It drove Combe out of his mind, but less so than these Fridays. What did they drink with their dinner?

Something strong – at least for Winnie, since her voice quickly turned throaty and deep.

How could she let herself lose control the way she did? He had never imagined passion of such violence, such unrestrained animality.

And J.K.C., faceless, remained calm, self-possessed, speaking in a level, almost patronizing voice.

After each new outburst she drank again; she shouted for something to drink. He pictured the studio in shambles, glasses shattered on the black floor.

This time he'd gone out without waiting for what always came next, the frantic comings and goings from the bathroom, the hiccupping, the vomiting, the tears. And, finally, that unending wail of a sick animal or a hysterical woman.

Why did he keep thinking about her? Why had he gone out? He had promised himself that one morning he'd be there in the hallway or on the stairs when she left. But every time, she managed to get up at seven sharp. She didn't need an alarm clock. She didn't bother to wake her friend. Combe never heard them talking in the morning.

Stray sounds from the bathroom, perhaps a kiss on the forehead for the man lying asleep, then she opened the door and slipped out. He imagined her searching briskly for a taxi to take her back to the station.

What did she look like in the morning? Could you make out the night's traces on her face, in her sagging shoulders, her hoarse voice?

That was the woman he wanted to see – not the one who got off the train, brimming with self-confidence, who then showed up at the studio as if she was just dropping in on some friends.

He wanted to see the woman at daybreak, when she went off alone, leaving the man asleep, selfish, stupefied, his damp forehead grazed by her lips.

He came to a corner that seemed vaguely familiar. A club was closing. The last customers were out on the sidewalk, waiting in vain for a taxi. On the corner two men who'd been drinking were finding it hard to say good-bye. They shook hands, pulled apart, then immediately turned back for a final confidence or renewed protestations of friendship.

Combe, too, looked like he'd been in a bar, not like someone who'd just gotten up.

But he hadn't been drinking. He was sober. He hadn't been out listening to jazz. He'd spent the night in the desert of his bed.

A subway station, black and metallic, stood in the middle of the intersection. At last a yellow cab pulled up to the sidewalk and a dozen nightclub patrons rushed in its direction. Not without difficulty, the cab drove off again, empty. Perhaps nobody was going the right way.

Two wide streets, almost deserted, with garlands of luminous globes running down the sidewalks.

On the corner, its high windows lit violently, aggressively, with boastful vulgarity, was a sort of long glass cage where people could be seen as dark smudges and where he went in just so as not to be alone.

Stools anchored to the floor along an endless counter made of something cold and plastic. Two sailors swayed drunkenly, and one of them shook his hand solemnly, saying something Combe failed to understand.

It wasn't on purpose that he sat down beside the woman. He realized it only when the white-coated black waiter was standing in front of him, impatient for his order.

The place smelled of fairgrounds, of lazy crowds, of nights when you stayed out because you couldn't go to bed, and it smelled like New York, of its calm and brutal indifference.

Picking at random, he ordered grilled sausages. Then he looked at his neighbor and she looked at him. She had just been served fried eggs, but she hadn't touched them. She lit a cigarette slowly and deliberately, leaving a trace of her lipstick on the paper.

'You're French?'

She asked the question in French, a French that at first he thought betrayed no accent.

'How'd you know?'

'I didn't. As soon as you came in, even before you said anything, I just thought you were French.'

She added, a hint of nostalgia in her smile, 'Paris?'

'Yes.'

'Which part?'

Did she see his eyes dim slightly?

'I had a villa in Saint-Cloud . . . You've been there?'

She recited, as they do on the Paris riverboats, 'Pont de Sèvre, Saint-Cloud, Point-du-Jour . . .'

Then, in a lower voice: 'I lived in Paris for six years. Do you know the church in Auteuil? My apartment was next door, on the corner of rue Mirabeau, a few steps from the Molitor swimming pool.'

How many people were in this diner? Ten at most, set apart from one another by empty stools and by another emptiness, indefinable and hard to pierce, which perhaps emanated from each of them.

Two black men in white overcoats linked them together – nothing else. From time to time one of the two men would turn to a kind of trap and take out a plate of something hot, before sliding it down the counter to one of the customers.

Why, despite the blinding brightness, did everything look gray? It was as if the painfully sharp lights were helpless to dispel all the darkness the people had brought in from the night outside.

'You're not eating?' he said, since silence had fallen.

'I'm in no hurry.'

She smoked like American women – the same gestures, the same pouting lips you saw on magazine covers and in movies. She struck the same poses, too, shrugging her fur coat off her shoulders to reveal her black silk dress, crossing her long legs in their sheer stockings.

He didn't need to turn to check her out. A mirror ran the length of the diner, and they could see themselves sitting side by side. The image was unflattering, almost distorted.

'You're not eating, either,' she said. 'Have you been in New York long?'

'About six months.'

What made him introduce himself just then? His vanity, of course – he was sure he was going to regret it.

'François Combe.' His voice as he said it wasn't nearly casual enough.

She must have heard him. She didn't seem surprised. And yet she'd lived in France.

'When were you in Paris?'

'Let's see ... The last time was three years ago. I passed through on my way from Switzerland, but didn't stay long.'

Immediately, she added, 'You've been to Switzerland?'

Without waiting for a reply, she said, 'I spent two winters at a sanatorium in Leysin.'

Strangely, it was those words that made him look at her for the first time as a woman. She went on with a show of gaiety that somehow touched him, 'It's not as terrible as people think. At least not for the ones who get out. They told me I was definitely cured.'

She stubbed out her cigarette in an ashtray and again he looked at the bloodlike stain her lips had left on it. For the space of a second, he thought of Winnie, though he'd never laid eyes on her.

It was the voice, he realized suddenly. This woman, whose name he didn't know, had one of Winnie's voices, the voice of her tragic moments, wounded and animal.

A low voice that made you think of a scar that hadn't healed, of a hurt that lingers beneath consciousness, soft and familiar, deep inside.

She ordered something from the black man and Combe frowned, for she'd used the same intonation, the same facial expression, the same fluid seductiveness she'd used on him.

'Your eggs will get cold,' he said testily.

What was he hoping for? Why did he want to get away from this room where a dirty mirror reflected their two images back at them?

Was he hoping they'd leave together, just like that, though they were total strangers?

She began to eat her eggs so slowly that it annoyed him. She stopped to shake pepper into the glass of tomato juice she had ordered.

It was like a movie in slow motion. One of the sailors was being sick in a corner, just as Winnie must be doing right now. His friend was helping him like a brother, while the black waiter looked on indifferently.

They had sat there a whole hour and still he knew nothing about her. It irritated him that she kept drawing things out.

In his mind, they'd already agreed to leave together, and her inexplicable stubbornness was cheating him of the little time they had.

Several minor problems were preoccupying him. Her accent, for one. Her French was perfect, but there was something about it he couldn't quite place.

When he asked her if she was American and she replied that she'd been born in Vienna, he understood.

'Here they call me Kay, but when I was little I was Katherine. Have you ever been to Vienna?'

'Yes.'

'Ah.'

She looked at him almost as he'd been looking at her. So she knew nothing about him, and he knew nothing about her. It was after four o'clock. From time to time someone came in from God knows where and with a tired sigh hoisted himself onto a stool.

She was still eating. She ordered a hideous cake covered with bright frosting that she picked at with the tip of her spoon. Just when he hoped she'd finished, she called the black man over and ordered coffee. It was scalding when it came, so they had to wait even longer.

'Give me a cigarette, won't you? I'm out.'

He knew she'd smoke it down to the end before leaving, maybe ask for another one, too. He was surprised at his own impatience.

Outside, wouldn't she simply offer him her hand and say good night?

At last they were outside. The corner was deserted except for a man who was asleep on his feet, with his back against the subway entrance. She didn't suggest a taxi. She started walking down the sidewalk as if it made perfect sense – as if it was taking her somewhere.

She stumbled a few times because of her high heels. After about a hundred yards, she took his arm, and it seemed like the two of them had been walking the streets of New York at five in the morning, from the beginning of time.

Later he'd remember the smallest details from that night, though while he was living it, it seemed so disjointed as to be unreal.

Fifth Avenue stretched on forever, but he only recognized it after ten blocks, when he saw the little church.

'I wonder if it's open,' Kay said and stopped.

Then, with unexpected sadness, she said, 'I'd be so happy if it were.'

She made him try all the doors to see if one was unlocked.

'A pity,' she said, sighing and taking his arm again.

Then, a bit farther on, 'My shoes are killing me.'

'Do you want to take a taxi?'

'No, let's walk.'

He didn't know her address and didn't ask her for it. It felt strange to be walking like this through the huge city without the slightest idea of where they were going or what would happen next.

He saw their reflection in a shop window. She was leaning on him a little, perhaps because she was tired, and he thought they looked like a pair of lovers, a sight that just the day before would have made him sick with loneliness.

He had gritted his teeth – especially the last few weeks – whenever he passed a couple that was so plainly a couple, almost reeking of intimacy.

And yet here they were, looking like a couple to anyone who saw them pass. A funny couple.

'Do you want a whiskey?' she suddenly asked.

'I didn't think there was anyplace open this time of night.'

But already she was off with this new notion of hers; she led him into a cross street.

'Wait . . . No, not here. On the next block.'

Nervously, she picked the wrong place twice, then pushed open the grilled door of a little bar where a light shone and a man with a mop stared back at them with startled eyes. She questioned him, and after another fifteen minutes of roaming, they found themselves at last in a basement where three gloomy men were drinking at a counter. She knew the place. She called the bartender Jimmy, but then remembered his name was Teddy. She launched into a long explanation of her mistake, though the bartender couldn't have cared less. She talked about some people she'd been here with before. The man listened without saying a thing.

It took her nearly half an hour to drink one scotch, and then she wanted another. She lit another cigarette. It was always going to be the last cigarette.

'As soon as I finish,' she promised, 'we can go.'

She grew chatty. Once outside, her grip on Combe's arm was tighter. She nearly tripped as she stepped onto the curb.

She talked about her daughter. She had a daughter somewhere in Europe, but it was hard to tell where, or why they were no longer together.

They reached Fifty-second, and they could see the lights of Broadway, where silhouetted crowds were streaming along the sidewalks.

It was almost six. They had walked a long way. They were both tired. Out of the blue Combe asked, 'Where do you live?'

She stopped and looked at him, and at first he thought she was angry. He was wrong, he saw at once. There was trouble, perhaps even real distress there. He realized he didn't even know what color her eyes were.

She took several hurried steps on her own, as though running away. Then she stopped and waited for him to catch up.

'Since this morning,' she said, looking him in the face, her expression tight, 'I don't live anywhere.'

Why was he so touched that he wanted to cry? They were standing in front of a shop, their legs so tired they were trembling, with a bitter, early-morning taste in their mouths and an aching emptiness in their heads.

Had the two whiskeys put them on edge?

It was ridiculous. Though they were both teary-eyed, they looked like they were scowling at each other. The gesture seemed sentimental, and yet he seized both her hands.

'Come on,' he said.

After a moment's hesitation, he added, 'Come on, Kay.'

It was the first time he'd spoken her name.

She asked, already yielding, 'Where are we going?'

He had no idea. He couldn't take her to his place, to that hole in the wall he hated, to the room that hadn't been cleaned for a week, with its unmade bed.

Again they started walking. Now that she had confessed she had nowhere to live, he was afraid of losing her.

She talked. She told a complicated story filled with first names that meant nothing to him but that she dropped as though anyone would know them.

'I was sharing Jessie's apartment. You should know Jessie! She's the most seductive woman I've ever met . . . Three years ago, her husband, Ronald, got a very important job in Panama. Jessie tried to live with him down there, but because of her health she couldn't . . . She came back to New York, it was okay with Ronald, and we took an apartment together. It was in Greenwich Village, not far from where you and I met.'

He was listening, but at the same time he was trying to solve the problem of the hotel. They were still walking. They were so tired they could barely feel it anymore.

'Jessie had a lover, a Chilean named Enrico, who's married, with two children. He was about to get a divorce for her . . . You know?'

Of course. But he was only vaguely following the story.

'Somebody must have told Ronald, and I think I know who. I'd just gone out this morning when he showed up. Enrico's pajamas and bathrobe were still hanging in the closet . . . It must have been a terrible scene. Ronald is the kind of man who stays calm no matter what, but I hate to think what he must be like when he gets angry . . . When I came home at two in the afternoon, the door was locked. A neighbor heard me knocking. Before Ronald took her away, Jessie managed to leave a letter for me. It's here in my purse . . .'

She wanted to open her purse and show him the letter. They had just crossed Sixth Avenue when Combe had stopped under a bright hotel sign. The sign was neon, a horrible purple-violet: Lotus Hotel.

He nudged Kay into the lobby. More than ever he seemed to be afraid. He spoke in a hushed voice to the night clerk leaning on his counter, who gave him a key on a brass disc.

The clerk took them up in a tiny elevator that smelled like a rest room. Kay squeezed Combe's arm and said in

French, 'You should ask him to get us some whiskey. I'm sure he can.'

Only later did he realize she'd called him *tu*.

It was about that time in the morning when Winnie got up without making a sound, leaving J.K.C.'s damp bed and slipping into the bathroom.

The room at the Lotus was as grimy as the daylight filtering through the curtains.

Kay had dropped into a chair, pushing her fur off her shoulders. She had mechanically kicked off her black suede shoes with the too-high heels. Now they were lying on the carpet.

She held a glass in her hand and was drinking slowly, staring into space. Her purse was open on her lap. There was a run, like a long scar, in one of her stockings.

'Pour me another, will you? It'll be the last.'

Already she looked a bit tipsy. She drank this glass faster than usual, then sat for a moment, shut up within herself, far away from the room and the man who was waiting without knowing exactly what he was waiting for.

At last she stood up, her big toes showing through her flesh-colored stockings. She turned her head away for a fraction of a second, then, with a gesture so simple it might have been practiced, she took two steps toward him, spread her arms to enfold his shoulders, raised herself on her toes, and drew his mouth to hers.

The cleaning staff in the corridor had just plugged in their vacuum cleaners. Downstairs the night clerk was getting ready to go home.

2

The surprising thing was that he felt almost glad not to find her there beside him, though an hour, even a few minutes later, the thought would have struck him as incredible, almost monstrous. But the thought hadn't been conscious, so he could deny, without being entirely dishonest, having committed this first betrayal.

When he woke up the room was dark, its darkness pierced by two shafts of reddish light. They were like wedges driven in through the curtains by the neon signs in the street.

He had stretched out his hand and touched nothing but the cold sheets.

Had he really been glad? Hadn't he really believed that things would be easier if they had ended like that?

Apparently not – because when he saw the crack of light under the bathroom door, his heart registered the shock.

What happened next happened so easily and naturally that he could barely recall the sequence of events.

He had climbed out of bed, he remembered, because he wanted a cigarette. She must have heard his footsteps on the carpet. She had opened the bathroom door while she was still in the shower.

'Do you know what time it is?' she asked happily.

Strangely ashamed of his nakedness, he'd reached for his shorts. 'No.'

'My sweet Frank, it is half-past seven in the evening.'

No one had ever called him that before, and the words made him feel lighter. It was a lightness that would stay with him for hours, and it made everything seem so easy that he had the wonderful impression he was juggling with life itself.

What had happened? It didn't matter. Nothing would matter anymore.

He said, 'I wonder how I'll shave.'

And she said, more tenderly than sarcastically, 'Just tell the bellboy to go out and get you a razor and some shaving cream. Do you want me to call him?'

She thought it was funny. She had woken up clear-headed, while he was still confused. This reality seemed so new that he wasn't too sure that it was, in fact, real.

He remembered, now, the tone of her voice when she had said, with some satisfaction, 'You're not fat.'

He replied, as seriously as he could, 'I've always played sports.'

And he almost flexed his muscles.

Strange, they'd gone to sleep in this room as the night ended and woken up again as the night began. He was almost afraid to leave it – frightened of forgetting some part of himself there that he might never be able to find again.

What was stranger still was that neither of them had thought of kissing. They both got dressed without embarrassment. She said thoughtfully, 'I should buy another pair of stockings.'

She licked her finger and drew it down the run he'd noticed the night before.

He asked, almost awkwardly, 'Can I borrow your comb?'

The street, which had been empty when they arrived, was noisy now, bustling, full of bars, restaurants, and shops that they hadn't noticed before.

Everything seemed even more delicious because of this unlikely solitude, together with a feeling of relaxation they seemed to have stolen from the Broadway crowds.

'You haven't forgotten anything?'

They were waiting for the elevator; the attendant wasn't the clerk from last night but a young girl in uniform, sullen and unresponsive. An hour later, no doubt, the clerk would have been back at his post: he would have understood.

Downstairs, Combe went to turn in the key at the desk, while Kay, calm and poised, waited for him a few steps away, like a wife or longtime lover.

'You keeping the room?'

Without thinking he said yes. He spoke quickly and quietly, not just because of her, but out of a sort of superstition. He didn't want to tempt fate by seeming, so early on, to guess the future.

What did he know about the future? They knew nothing about each other, even less than last night, perhaps. And yet had two beings, two human bodies, ever plunged into each other with such savagery, with such desperate fury?

He didn't remember how they'd fallen asleep or when. At one point he woke up and it was broad daylight. He had seen her, a pained expression on her face, her body almost spread-eagled, one foot and one hand hanging down to the floor. She hadn't even opened her eyes as he rearranged her in the bed.

Now they were outside, turning their backs on the Lotus's purple neon sign, and Kay again took his arm as she had during their long walk through the night.

But now he resented her for having taken his arm the day before, for having taken the arm of a stranger so soon, so easily.

'Maybe we could grab something to eat?' she asked in a joking tone.

Joking because everything seemed like a joke to them, because they were being knocked around by the crowd as lightly as Ping-Pong balls.

'You want some dinner?'

She burst out laughing. 'Shouldn't we have breakfast first?'

He no longer knew who he was or how old he was. He no longer recognized the city he had stalked, bitterly and warily, for six months, and whose overwhelming lack of coherence suddenly filled him with wonder.

This time she led the way as if it were the most natural thing in the world. He asked meekly, 'Where are we going?'

'To the cafeteria in Rockefeller Center.'

They had already reached the main building. Kay found her way easily through the vast corridors of gray marble, and for the first time he was jealous. It was ridiculous.

Anxiously, like a teenager, he asked, 'Do you come here often?'

'Sometimes. When I'm in the neighborhood.'

'With who?'

'Idiot.'

So in one night, in less than one night, they had miraculously run through a cycle that lovers can take weeks or months to complete.

He was surprised to find himself eyeing the boy who took their order to make sure he didn't know her, that she hadn't come here a hundred times with other men. Would he make some sign of recognition to her?

Yet he wasn't in love with her. He was sure he wasn't. Already he felt irritation watching her fumble in her purse for a cigarette, with her commonplace gestures, the way she brought the cigarette up to her lips, smudging it with her lipstick as she fished around for her lighter.

She would finish her cigarette, he knew, whether or not her food arrived. She'd light another – many others, probably – before deciding to swallow down the last drop of coffee in her cup. And she'd smoke another cigarette before leaving and put on some more lipstick. She'd pout slightly, with annoying seriousness, at the mirror she carried in her purse.

But he sat through it. He couldn't imagine doing anything else. He waited, resigned to it, resigned to whatever else might come, and he caught sight of himself in a mirror, his smile at once tense and childish. That smile reminded him of high school, when he would torture himself with thoughts about whether or not some girl would go to bed with him.

He was forty-eight years old.

He hadn't told her. They hadn't talked about their ages. Would he tell her the truth? Would he say he was forty? Forty-two?

Who knew, anyway, if they'd still be together in an hour, in half an hour?

Was that why they were killing time, why they had been killing time since they'd met – because there was no reason to believe that they had any future together at all?

The street again, where they felt easiest with each other. Their moods brightened; they rediscovered the miraculous lightness they had stumbled on earlier by chance.

People were lining up in front of the movie theaters. Some of the velvet-covered doors guarded by men in uniforms must have led into nightclubs.

They didn't go into any. They didn't even think about it. They traced their way, zigzagging through the crowds, until Kay turned to him with a smile he knew at once.

Wasn't that the smile that had started everything?

He wanted to say to her, as to a child, before she even opened her mouth, 'Yes . . .'

Because he knew. And she understood that he knew. The proof was that she said, 'Just one, all right?'

They didn't bother looking around, and at the first corner they pushed open the door of a little bar. It was so intimate, so cozy, so made to order for lovers that it seemed to have been set down in their path on purpose. Kay said to him with a look: 'See?'

Then, holding out her hand, she whispered, 'Give me a nickel.'

Not understanding, he gave her the coin. He saw her, at one end of the bar, approach a huge, round-edged machine containing an automatic turntable and a stack of records.

She looked more serious than he'd ever seen her. Frowning, she read the titles of the records on the metal tabs and at last found what she was looking for; she pressed a button and came back and climbed onto her barstool.

'Two scotches.'

She waited, a vague smile on her lips, for the first notes, and at that moment he felt a second twinge of jealousy. Who had she been with, where and when had she first heard the piece she'd looked for so long?

He glowered stupidly at the incurious bartender.

'Just listen . . . don't make that face, darling.'

The machine stood bathed in orange light, and out of it, very softly, almost like someone telling a secret, came one of those melodies that, whispered by a tenderly insinuating voice, would nurse thousands of romances for six months or a year.

She took his arm. She squeezed it. She smiled at him, and for the first time her smile showed her teeth, too white, almost frail in their whiteness.

He tried to say something.

'Hush,' she said.

A bit later, she said, 'Give me another nickel, will you?'

To replay the same song, the one they would listen to seven or eight times that night, drinking whiskeys, saying almost nothing to each other.

'You're not bored?'

No – he wasn't at all bored, and yet something strange was happening. He wanted to be with her. He only felt good when she was beside him. He dreaded the moment of separation. At the same time, as in the cafeteria, or like the night in the diner or in the bar where they finally ended up, he felt an almost physical impatience.

The music finally got to him, too, with its almost hurrying gentleness, but still he wanted it over. He told himself, *After this one, we go*.

He resented Kay for interrupting their aimless and pointless wandering.

She asked, 'What do you want to do?'

He didn't know. He had no sense of time, of everyday life. He didn't want to return to it, though he was plagued by an indefinable sense of uneasiness that prevented him from giving himself up to the moment.

'Would you mind walking around Greenwich Village?'

What did it matter? He was very happy, and he was very unhappy. Outside, she hesitated for an instant, and he knew why. It was amazing how they were aware of even the slightest nuance in each other's mood.

She was wondering if they'd take a taxi. The question of money had never come up between them. She didn't know whether he was rich or poor, and she had been startled, a moment earlier, by the size of the check for the whiskeys.

He raised his arm. A yellow cab stopped at the curb in front of them, and then, like thousands of other couples at the same instant, they were in the soft shadows of the car, with multicolored lights playing on the driver's back.

He saw her taking off a glove. She slipped her bare hand into his, and they remained that way, motionless, silent, during the whole trip down to Washington Square. They were no longer in noisy, anonymous New York, but in a neighborhood that looked like any other small town in the world.

The sidewalks were empty, and there were not many shops. A couple appeared from a side street, the man awkwardly pushing a stroller.

'I'm glad you wanted to come downtown. I've been so happy here.'

He was frightened. He wondered if she was going to start talking about herself. Inevitably she would sometime, and then he'd have to do the same.

But not now. She was silent. She had a way of leaning gently against his arm, and there was another gesture he'd never known her to make before, that he'd never seen anyone make: as they walked she'd brush her cheek against his so fleetingly he was scarcely aware of it.

'Shall we turn left here?'

They were five minutes from his place, the room where, he suddenly remembered, he had left the light on.

He laughed to himself. She sensed it: already they could hide nothing from each other.

'What are you laughing at?'

He was going to tell her. Then he realized she'd want to see his place.

'It's nothing. I don't know what came over me.'

She stopped on the sidewalk in a street full of three-and four-story houses.

'Look,' she said. She stared at a house with a white facade and several windows lighted. 'That's where I lived with Jessie.'

Farther down the street, past a Chinese laundry, was a basement-level Italian restaurant with red-and-white-checked curtains.

'We used to have dinner there, the two of us.'

She counted the windows and added, 'There, fourth floor, second and third windows from the right. It's pretty small, you know – just one bedroom, the living room, and a bathroom.'

He felt hurt – as he'd expected.

Resenting her, he asked almost harshly, 'What did you do when Enrico came to see your friend?'

'I slept on the sofa in the living room.'

'Every time?'

'What do you mean?'

Now he knew he was on to something. Kay hesitated a moment before replying. She'd answered a question with a question, which meant she felt embarrassed.

He was furious. Thinking of the paper-thin wall that separated him from Winnie and J.K.C., he said, 'You know very well what I mean.'

'Let's keep walking.'

The two of them alone in the deserted neighborhood. With the feeling that they had nothing else to say to each other.

'Shall we go in here?'

A little bar, another, one she must know, since it was on her street. What the hell. He said yes and immediately regretted it, since it didn't have the intimacy of the bar they'd just left. The room was too big, it smelled of piss, the counter was filthy, the glasses scratched and clouded.

'Two scotches.'

Then she said, 'Don't worry. Give me a nickel.'

Here, too, was an enormous jukebox, but she searched in vain for their song. She chose something at random while a stranger drunkenly tried to start a conversation.

They finished their pale, lukewarm whiskeys.

'Let's get out of here.'

On the street again, she said, 'You know, I never slept with Ric.'

He almost sneered – now she was calling him Ric instead of Enrico. But what did it matter? Hadn't she obviously slept with other men before?

'He tried, one night, I think. I'm not really sure.'

Didn't she realize the best thing would be to shut up? Was she doing it on purpose? He wanted to take his arm back, to walk by himself, hands in his pockets, to light a cigarette or better still his pipe, something he hadn't yet done in front of her.

'I want you to know, so you don't start getting ideas. Ric is South American, you understand? One night . . . it was two months ago, well, in August . . . It was very hot.

Have you been in New York during a heat wave? The apartment was like a furnace.'

They'd come back to Washington Square. They circled around it slowly, a void between them. Why was she still talking when he was pretending not to hear her?

Why, worst of all, was she bringing images he knew he'd never be able to erase from his mind? He wanted to order her to shut up. Didn't women have any shame at all?

'All he had on were his pants . . . He looked good, you know.'

'And you?'

'What about me?'

'What were you wearing?'

'A nightgown, I suppose. I don't remember . . . Yes, Jessie and I must have been wearing nightgowns.'

'But you were naked underneath.'

'Probably.'

She still didn't seem to understand. But she had enough presence of mind to stop in the middle of the square, turn, and say, 'I forgot to show you Mrs Roosevelt's house. You know the one? That's it, over there, on the corner. When he was in the White House, the President would sneak off to spend a few days or hours there, unknown to anyone, even the Secret Service.'

She came back to her subject. 'That night . . .'

He almost twisted her wrist to shut her up.

'That night, I remember wanting to go into the bathroom to take a shower. Ric was restless, I don't know why. Well, I think I do know, looking back. He said we were all idiots, that we'd be better off getting undressed and taking a shower together . . . You see?'

'And you did?' he said spitefully.

'I took a shower alone, and I locked the door. Ever since, I refused to go out with him unless Jessie came, too.'

'But you'd gone out with him alone before?'

'Why not?'

Then she asked, with all apparent innocence, 'What are you thinking about?'

'Nothing. Everything.'

'Are you jealous of Ric?'

'No.'

'Listen. Have you ever been to the Number One bar?'

Suddenly he felt very tired. For a moment he was so sick of walking around the streets with her that he was ready to leave her at the first opportunity. What were they doing, clinging to each other as though they'd always been in love and were destined to love each other forever?

Enrico . . . Ric . . . the three of them in the shower. She was lying. He sensed it, he knew it. She couldn't have resisted something like that.

She was lying, not on purpose but because she needed to, just like she needed to look at every man who went by, using her smile to win the homage of a bartender, a waiter, a taxi driver.

'Did you see the way he was looking at me?'

She had said that a little while before – about the taxi driver who had brought them to Greenwich Village, who'd probably barely noticed them, whose only thought was probably his tip.

Still, he followed her into a dimly lit room done in soft rose, where someone was casually playing the piano, letting his long pale fingers play over the keys, scattering notes that created an atmosphere thick with nostalgia.

She stopped in the doorway and said, 'Leave your coat in the cloakroom.'

As though he didn't know! She led the way. She was glowing. She crossed the room behind the maître d', an excited smile on her lips.

She must have thought herself beautiful, but she wasn't. What he really liked about her were the signs of wear and tear on her face, her eyelids with their tiny wrinkles like onionskin and occasional traces of purple, or at other times, the fatigue that dragged down the corners of her mouth.

'Two scotches.'

She had to speak to the maître d', to practice on him what she imagined to be her powers of seduction. She was solemn as she asked him pointless questions, what numbers they'd missed in the floor show, what had become of a singer she'd seen there a few months back.

She lit a cigarette, of course, shrugged her fur off her shoulders, tilted her head back, sighed with pleasure.

'You're not happy?'

He was in a bad mood. 'Why would I be unhappy?' he replied.

'I don't know. Right now I think you hate me.'

How sure she must be of herself to state the truth so simply, so bluntly! Sure of what? Because, after all, what kept him from leaving her? What kept him from just going home?

He didn't find her seductive. She wasn't beautiful. She wasn't even young. And she'd obviously known more than enough men.

Was that what drew him to her and moved him so much?

'Will you excuse me for a minute?'

She glided over to the pianist. Her smile, once more, was that of a woman automatically bent on seduction, who would be outraged if the beggar she gave a few cents to on the street refused her a look of admiration.

She returned to the table, beaming, eyes sparkling with irony, and she was right, in a sense, since it was on his behalf – at least on their behalf – that she had tried to be charming.

The fingers running over the keyboard shifted cadences, and now it was the melody from the little bar that thrummed in the rose-tinted dimness. She listened to it, lips half parted, the smoke from her cigarette drifting up in front of her face like incense.

As soon as the melody ended, she made a small nervous gesture. Then she stood up, gathered her cigarettes, lighter, and gloves, and told him, 'Pay the check. Let's go.'

She turned to him as he fumbled in his pocket and said, 'You always tip too much. Forty cents is plenty here.'

More than anything else, it was taking possession, taking it quietly, and without any argument. He said nothing.

At the cloakroom, she said, 'Leave a quarter.' And out-side, 'Let's not bother taking a taxi.'

To where? Was she so sure they were going to stay together? She didn't even know he'd kept their room at the Lotus, but he knew she was sure he had.

'Shall we take the subway?'

At least she'd asked for his opinion, and he replied, 'Not right away. I'd rather walk for a bit.'

Like the night before, they were at the bottom of Fifth Avenue, and already he wanted to do everything the same again. He wanted to walk with her, to turn the same cor-ners, maybe even to stop at that strange cellar where they had drunk whiskey together that first night.

She was tired, he knew. It was difficult for her to walk in her high heels. But the idea of revenge, of making her suffer a little, wasn't displeasing. He wondered if she'd complain. It was a kind of test.

'Whatever you like.'

Were they going to talk things over now? He wanted to, and he was afraid to. He wasn't in any more of a hurry to learn about Kay's life than he was to talk about his own, above all to tell her who he was, since at heart it pained him to be taken for just anyone, even more to be loved as just anyone.

The night before, she hadn't blinked when he told her his name. Perhaps she hadn't heard it right. Perhaps she hadn't connected the name of the man she had met in Manhattan at three in the morning with the name she had seen in big letters plastered on the walls of Paris.

They passed a Hungarian restaurant and she asked, 'Have you ever been to Budapest?'

She wasn't waiting for an answer. He answered that he had been to Budapest, but obviously it didn't matter. He felt a confused hope that at last this was a chance to talk about himself; instead she talked about herself.

'What a lovely city! I think I was happier there than anywhere else. I was sixteen.'

He frowned because she was talking about being sixteen, and he was afraid another Enrico was about come up.

'I was living with my mother. I'll show you a photo of her. She was the most beautiful woman I've ever seen.'

He wondered if she was chattering like this just to shut him up. What kind of idea did she have about him? The wrong one, no doubt. And yet she still clung to his arm eagerly.

'My mother was a famous pianist. You must have heard her name – she played in all the large cities: Miller . . . Edna Miller. Miller's my maiden name, since she never married. Do you find that shocking?'

'Me? No.'

He wanted to tell her that he was a great artist himself. He did, however, get married, which was why . . .

For a moment he closed his eyes. When he opened them, he saw himself as someone else might have, perhaps even more clearly, walking up Fifth Avenue with a woman clinging to his arm, a woman he didn't know and with whom he was headed God knew where.

She interrupted herself. 'Am I boring you?'

'Not at all.'

'Do you really want to hear about my childhood?'

Was he going to say yes or no? He didn't know any-more. What he did know was that when she spoke he felt a dull nagging pain in the left side of his chest.

Why? He had no idea. Because he wished his life had begun last night? Perhaps. But it didn't matter. Nothing mattered now, because he had suddenly decided to stop resisting.

He listened. He walked. He looked at the luminous globes of the streetlights angling off into infinity, at the taxis sliding silently by, almost always with a man and a woman inside.

Hadn't he burned with envy of all of those couples? Wanting a woman on his arm like Kay was now?

'Do you mind stopping here for a moment?'

It wasn't a bar this time, but a pharmacy, and she smiled at him. He understood her smile; she wanted to buy a few toiletries. He understood that she had just realized, as he had, how it marked another step in their growing intimacy.

She let him pay and he was happy to, just as he was happy to hear the clerk call her 'ma'am.'

'Now,' she decided, 'we can go back.'

He couldn't help asking, ironically, and he was sorry as soon as he did: 'Without one last scotch?'

'No more scotch,' she replied seriously. 'Tonight I'm more like that girl of sixteen. Do you mind?'

The night clerk remembered them. How could the fact of seeing the Lotus's crass purple sign, those few letters over its door, give such pleasure? And it was a pleasure, too, to be greeted as old customers by the shabby, tired-out clerk. To return to the banality of the hotel room and to see two pillows waiting on the made-up bed.

'Why don't you take off your coat and sit down?'

He obeyed. He was somehow touched, and maybe she was, too. He couldn't tell anymore. There were moments when he hated her and moments, like this one, when he wanted to put his head on her shoulder and cry.

He was tired but he felt relaxed. He waited, smiling a little, and she caught the smile and understood it, too, since she came over and kissed him for the first time that day, not greedily like the night before, not desperately, but very slowly bringing her lips close to his, hesitating before they touched, then pressing them tenderly together.

He closed his eyes. When he reopened them, he saw that hers were closed, too, and he was grateful.

'Let go of me now. Stay there.'

She switched off the overhead light, leaving on only the tiny lamp with its silk shade on the night table. Then she went to the cupboard for the bottle of whiskey they had opened the night before.

'It's not the same thing as going to a bar.'

Already he understood. She filled two glasses, measuring out the whiskey and water as carefully as if following a recipe. She set one glass before him, brushing his forehead with her hand as she did.

'Are you happy?'

Kicking off her shoes with a now familiar movement, she curled up in a big chair like a little girl.

Then she sighed, and in a voice he hadn't heard her use before said, 'I'm so happy!'

They were only a few feet apart, yet they both knew that neither would cross that space. They looked at each other, their eyes half closed, pleased to see in the other's face the same soft, peaceful light.

Was she going to start talking again?

Her lips parted, but only to sing, to barely murmur the song that was now their song.

And the little tune was so completely transformed that tears came to his eyes, his chest filled with warmth.

She knew it. She knew everything. She held him to her with the song, with the serious note in her voice, though it cracked now and then, and deftly she drew out their pleasure in being just the two of them, alone together, separate from the rest of the world.

When at last she finished, there was a silence that filled with the sounds drifting in off the street.

They listened to them with astonishment. Then she asked again, much more softly this time: 'Are you happy?'

Did he really say the words that came next, or did they simply echo inside him?

'I've never been happier in my life.'

3

It was an odd sensation. She was speaking. He was moved by what she was saying. But not for a moment did he lose his clarity of mind. He said to himself, *She's lying!*

He was sure she was lying. Maybe she wasn't making it all up, though he felt she was capable of that. But she was certainly lying by distorting, exaggerating, or leaving things out.

Two or three times she poured herself a drink. He stopped counting. He knew now that this was her hour and that the whiskey kept her going, and he pictured her on other nights, with other men, drinking to keep her spirits up, talking, endlessly talking, in that husky, alluring voice.

Did she tell them exactly the same things? Did she sound just as sincere?

What was most surprising was that he didn't care. He didn't hold it against her.

She told him about her husband, a Hungarian, Count Larski. She said she'd been married when she was nineteen. And already she told a lie, or half a lie, since she claimed she'd been a virgin. She went on about how brutal he'd been on their wedding night, forgetting that a little earlier she'd spoken about a romance she'd had at seventeen.

He was suffering, not because of the lies but because of the images they brought up. If he resented her for anything, it was for dirtying herself in his eyes with a shamelessness that bordered on insolence.

Was the whiskey making her talk like this? There were moments when he said to himself, coldly: *She's a three-o'-clock woman, a woman who never wants to go to bed, who has to keep her emotions at fever pitch no matter how, who has to drink, smoke, and talk until she falls into a man's arms out of sheer nervous exhaustion.*

And yet he stayed. He hadn't the slightest urge to run away. The more clear-sighted he became, the more he realized that Kay was indispensable to him, and he gave himself up to that fact.

That was it exactly. Gave himself up. He couldn't tell at what moment the decision had been made, but it was decided. He wouldn't struggle, no matter what he found out.

Why didn't she shut up? It would have been so simple. He would have put his arms around her. He would have whispered, 'We're starting all over again – none of that matters.'

Starting all over again from zero. The two of them. Two lives from zero.

From time to time she would break off, 'You're not listening.'

'Yes, I am.'

'You're listening, but you're thinking about something else at the same time.'

He was thinking about himself, her, everything. He was himself and someone watching himself. He loved her and still he judged her without mercy.

She said: 'We lived in Berlin for two years. My husband was an attaché at the Hungarian embassy. It was there, or more exactly in Swansee, by the lake, that my daughter was born. Her name is Michelle. Do you like the name Michelle?'

She didn't wait for an answer.

'Poor Michelle! She's with one of her aunts, a sister of Larski's who never married and who lives in a huge castle a hundred kilometers from Buda.'

He didn't like the huge romantic castle, which may or may not in fact have existed. He asked himself, *How many men has she told this story to?*

He scowled and she noticed.

'Is the story of my life boring you?'

'Not at all.'

It was probably all necessary, like the last cigarette he was anxiously waiting for her to stub out. He felt happy, but happy only for what lay ahead. He wanted to be done once and for all with the past and the present.

'Then he was appointed first secretary in Paris, and we had to live at the embassy because the ambassador was a widower and he needed a woman there for the receptions.'

She was lying. When she spoke to him the first time about Paris, in the diner, she said she'd lived by the Auteuil church in the rue Mirabeau. Hungary had never had an embassy in the rue Mirabeau.

She went on, 'Jean was quite a man, one of the most intelligent I'd ever met . . .'

And he was jealous. He resented her for dragging up yet another name.

'He was a great lord in his own country. You don't know Hungary –'

'Yes, I do.'

She swept aside the objection by impatiently flicking the ash off her cigarette.

'You can't. You're too French. I'm Viennese and have Hungarian blood in my veins on my grandmother's side, but even I couldn't. When I say a great lord, I don't mean a great lord like in the Middle Ages. I've seen him horse-whip his servants. One day when our driver nearly turned us over in the Black Forest, he knocked him down and beat him senseless. He said to me calmly, 'I'm sorry I don't have a revolver on me. That lout might have killed you.'

And still he lacked the nerve to tell her to shut up.

It seemed to him that this chatter demeaned them both, that she was demeaning herself by talking just as he was by listening.

'I was pregnant at the time, which explains his anger and brutality. He was so jealous that even a month before I gave birth, when no man would think of looking at me, he kept his eye on me day and night. I wasn't allowed to go out alone. He locked me in my rooms. He locked up all my shoes and clothes in one room and carried the key around with him.'

She didn't understand that it was all wrong, that it was even worse for her to explain. 'We lived in Paris for three years.'

Yesterday, she had said six years. Who was she with the rest of the time?

'The ambassador, who died last year, was one of our greatest statesmen, an old man of eighty-four. He was like a father to me, since he'd been a widower for thirty years and had no children.'

You're lying, he thought.

Because it was impossible. At least with her. The ambassador could have been ninety, he could have been a hundred, but she wouldn't have rested until she'd made him pay her homage.

'Often, at night, he'd ask me to read to him. It was one of the few pleasures he had left.'

He barely kept himself from shouting, 'Where were his hands while you were reading to him?' Because it was obvious to him, and it hurt.

Hurry up, he thought. *Get it all out so the whole rotten business can be forgotten.*

'Because of that, my husband claimed that the Paris air was bad for me, and we moved to a villa in Nogent. His mood got gloomier and gloomier, and he got more and more jealous. In the end, I couldn't stand it any more and ran away.'

All by yourself? Come on! If she had run away like that on her own, would she have left her daughter behind? If she had asked for a divorce, would she be where she was now?

He clenched his fists. He wanted to hit her, to avenge them both, him and the husband he utterly detested.

'Is that when you went to Switzerland?' he asked, barely disguising his sarcasm.

But she understood. He knew she did, since she replied curtly, without going into details: 'Not right away. First I lived on the Riviera and in Italy for a year.'

She didn't say who she had spent the year with, and didn't claim to have lived alone.

He hated her. He wanted to twist her arm back, forcing her to her knees so she would have to beg him to forgive her.

It was unbelievably ironic, this woman curled up in her chair declaring, with a kind of monstrous candor, 'There – I've told you my whole life story!'

But what about the rest, everything she hadn't said, everything she didn't want him to know? Didn't she realize that out of her whole story what stuck in his craw to the point of causing him physical pain was that she let herself be felt up by the old ambassador?

He rose mechanically and said, 'Come to bed.'

And, as he had expected, she whispered, 'Can I finish my cigarette?'

He snatched it out of her fingers and crushed it with his shoe on the rug.

'Come to bed.'

She was smiling, he knew, when she turned her head. She knew she'd won. To think she'd tell stories like that just to put him in the state she could see he was in!

I'm not going to touch her tonight, he promised himself. *That way maybe she'll understand.*

Understand what? It was absurd. But then, wasn't this whole thing absurd and meaningless? What were they doing, the two of them, in a room at the Lotus, above a purple neon sign designed to attract straying couples?

He watched her take her clothes off, and he remained cold. Yes, he could remain cold to her. She wasn't beautiful or irresistible, as she thought she was. Her body, like her face, was marked by life.

And now, thinking about her, he felt himself carried away by anger, by a need to wipe out everything, to consume everything, to possess everything. Furiously, with an animus that fixed his pupils in a terrifying stare, he grabbed her, threw her down, and thrust into her as though wanting to exorcise his obsession once and for all.

She watched him, bewildered with fear, and when the spasm was spent she cried, not like Winnie on the other side of the wall, but like a child. Like a child she stammered, 'You hurt me.'

Like a child, she fell asleep almost immediately. And that night, unlike the previous one, there was no look of pain on her face. This time she lay calm. She slept, her lower lip slightly protruding, her arms stretched limply on the blanket, her hair in a tangled auburn mass against the stark whiteness of the pillow.

He didn't sleep, didn't even try. Dawn wasn't far off, and when its first cold gleam touched the window, he slid behind the curtains to cool his forehead against the glass.

No one was in the street. The trash cans gave it a look of banal intimacy. Across the way, on the same story, a man was shaving at a mirror hooked to his window frame. For an instant their eyes met.

What would they say to each other? They were about the same age. The man across the way was balding and had thick, worried-looking eyebrows. Was there someone behind him in the room, a woman still asleep in the bed?

A man up so early must be leaving for work. What did he do? What path was his life following?

For months now, Combe's life had been going nowhere. But, until two days ago, he had at least been walking stubbornly in one direction.

On this chilly October morning, he was a man who had cut all the threads, a man approaching fifty, without ties to anything – not to family, profession, country, himself, and definitely not to a home. His only connection was to a complete stranger, a woman sleeping in his room in a seedy hotel.

A light was on in the window across the way, and it made him think of the light that was still burning at his own place. Perhaps it was just an excuse, a pretext.

Wouldn't he, sooner or later, have to go home? Kay would sleep all day; he was beginning to know her. He'd leave a note on the bedside table telling her he'd be back soon.

He would go to Greenwich Village and straighten up his room. Maybe he'd find a way to clean it.

He dressed silently in the bathroom, with the door closed behind him, and his mind was already working. Not only would he clean his room from top to bottom, he'd also go out and buy flowers. And he'd buy a cheap cretonne bedspread, brightly colored, to put over his gray blanket. Then he'd order in a cold supper from the Italian restaurant that served J.K.C. and Winnie every week.

He would need to call the radio station, since he had a broadcast scheduled for the next day. He should have called already.

Tired though he was, he was suddenly full of determination. He looked forward to the prospect of a brisk walk alone, hearing his footsteps echo on the empty sidewalks, breathing in the crisp morning air.

Kay slept. He watched her, her lower lip still protruding, and he smiled, almost condescendingly. Yes, she had found a place in his life. What point was there, right now, in measuring the importance of that place?

If he hadn't been afraid of waking her, he would have kissed her gently on the forehead.

'I'll be back soon,' he wrote on a blank page in his notebook. He tore it out and slipped it under her cigarette case.

And that made him smile, too. He knew she'd find it there.

In the hallway he filled his pipe. Before lighting it, he pressed the elevator button.

The night clerk was off already; one of the girls in uniform was running the car. He went out without stopping at the desk and paused at the curb to fill his lungs.

'Finally,' he almost sighed.

He nearly wondered if he'd ever come back.

He took a few steps, stopped, then walked a little farther.

Suddenly he felt anxious, like a man who has forgotten something but can't remember what.

He stopped again at the corner of Broadway, where the extinguished lights and too-wide sidewalks sent a chill through him.

What would he do if the room was empty when he returned?

The thought had barely struck him, and already it hurt. It put him in such confusion, such a state of panic, that he turned around quickly to make sure no one was leaving the hotel.

A few seconds later at the entrance to the Lotus, he knocked out his still-lit pipe against his heel.

'Eighth floor, please,' he told the girl who had just brought him down in the elevator.

And he only relaxed when he saw Kay still asleep. Nothing in their room had changed.

He didn't know if she'd seen him leave or come back. It was a moment of such deep and mixed emotion that he would never dare to tell her about it. She appeared to be asleep as he got undressed and slipped back under the covers.

Still apparently asleep, she sought out his body with her own.

She didn't open her eyes. Her eyelids fluttered a bit but didn't open, and they made him think of a great bird beating its wings but somehow unable to take flight.

Her voice was heavy and distant but without reproach or sadness as she said, 'You tried to run away, didn't you?'

And he almost responded, which would have ruined everything. Luckily she continued in the same voice, though fainter now, 'You couldn't.'

Then she was asleep. Maybe she hadn't really woken up, and it was only from the bottom of some deep dream that she had been aware of the drama that had just taken place.

Much later, when they woke up, she didn't say a thing.

Already it felt as though they'd lived through a thousand similar mornings. It seemed impossible that this was only the second time they'd woken up together, naked and intimate, as if they'd been lovers forever.

Even the room at the Lotus seemed familiar. They were surprised how much they liked it.

'I'll run to the bathroom first.'

Then she had the remarkable insight to say, 'Why don't you ever smoke your pipe? You can, you know. I don't mind. In Hungary there are a lot of women who smoke pipes.'

That morning they seemed newly minted. Their eyes shone with a pure, almost childlike happiness. They were playing at life.

'When I think that because of Ronald I'll probably never get my things back again! I have two trunks full of clothes there, and now I can't even change stockings.'

She laughed. How wonderful to feel so light waking up, to stand at the threshold of a new day with no constraints, a day you could fill up with whatever you felt like.

The sun was out, a bright, sparkling sun. They went to a diner for breakfast. Already that was one of their habits.

'You feel like taking a walk in Central Park?'

He didn't want to be jealous; their day had only just begun. But each time she proposed doing something, whenever she mentioned some place or other, he couldn't help asking himself, *Who was she with before?*

Who had she gone to Central Park with? What memories was she trying to relive?

That morning she looked young. And probably because she also felt young she said, very seriously, as they walked together, 'You know, I'm already quite old. I'm thirty-two. Soon I'll be thirty-three.'

Her daughter, he calculated, must be about twelve, and he paid attention now to the little girls playing in the park.

'I'm forty-eight,' he confessed. 'Well, not quite. I will be in a month.'

'Men don't age.'

Was this the moment to open up about himself? He hoped so, but he was scared, too.

What would happen when they finally had to look reality in the face?

Up to now they had been outside of real life, but the time would come when they would have to go back, whether they liked it or not.

Did she know what he was thinking? Her naked hand found his, as in the taxi, and gave a gentle squeeze, as if to say, 'Not yet.'

He had made up his mind to take her to his place, and he was afraid. Leaving the Lotus, he'd paid the bill for the room. She had noticed, but she hadn't said a word.

That might mean a lot of things. Maybe this would be their last walk together – at least their last before they reentered reality.

Maybe that was why she had suggested this stroll, arm in arm, in Central Park, in the warm fall sun – to provide them with one last radiant memory.

She began humming their song, the tune from the little bar. They both had the same thought. Night began to fall and it cooled down. The shadows on the path grew darker. They looked at each other without speaking; they knew what they wanted to do. They headed toward Sixth Avenue.

They didn't take a taxi. They walked. It was their fate, and they were afraid to do anything else. Most of the time they'd been together – and it seemed a long time now – they'd spent on sidewalks, walking, jostled by crowds they barely noticed.

The time was coming when they would have to stop walking and still they kept putting it off.

'Listen . . .'

At times she moved with a kind of childish joy. When that happened, he thought that fate must be on their side. They walked into the little bar, and the jukebox was playing their song. A sailor, elbows on the bar, was staring intently at nothing.

Kay squeezed Combe's arm and glanced feelingly at the man who'd picked their song to accompany his sadness.

'Give me a nickel,' she whispered.

She played the song three times in a row. The sailor turned his head and smiled sadly. Gulping his drink down, he staggered out, bumping into the door frame on the way.

'Poor man!' she said.

He almost wasn't jealous, but he was, a bit. He had to talk, he wanted to more and more, and yet he didn't dare.

Was she deliberately refusing to help?

Again she was drinking, but he didn't mind. Mechanically he drank with her. He was very sad and he was very happy, feeling an emotion so keen that he teared up when he heard a phrase from their song or just looked around their bar, drowned in muted light.

That night, they walked. For a long time they wandered through the crowds on Broadway and went into bar after bar without ever finding the atmosphere of their favorite spot.

They'd go in, order drinks. Invariably, Kay lit a cigarette. She'd touch his elbow, saying, 'Look.'

And she'd point to an unhappy couple lost in thought, or a lone woman getting drunk.

She seemed to be seeking out the despair of others, as if she wanted to rub against it, to wear it down before it could pierce her.

'Let's go.'

They looked at each other and smiled. They had uttered these words so many times, though in fact they had only been together two days and two nights.

'Funny, isn't it?'

He didn't have to ask her what was funny. They were thinking the same thing, two people who didn't know each other and who had come together by a miracle in the great city, and who now clung desperately to each other, as if already they felt a chilly solitude settling in.

Soon . . . later, Combe thought.

On Twenty-fourth Street there was a little Chinese shop with a sign over it advertising baby turtles for sale.

'Buy me one, will you?'

They put it into a little cardboard box, and Kay carried it carefully, forcing out a laugh. She was probably thinking that it was the only pledge of love between them.

'Listen, Kay . . .'

She put a finger to her lips.

'I need to tell you . . .'

'Hush! Let's get something to eat.'

They lingered amid the city. They did it deliberately. It was in a crowd that they felt happiest.

She ate as she had the first night, but her slowness no longer bothered him.

'There are so many other things to tell you! I know what you think about me. But you're wrong, Frank, you're wrong.'

It was two in the morning, later perhaps, and they were walking back down Fifth Avenue, a distance they'd already covered twice.

'Where are you taking me?'

No sooner had she said it than she changed her mind. 'No, don't tell.'

He didn't know what he was going to do, what he was hoping for. He stared straight ahead as he walked. For once, she kept silent, too.

And gradually, this silent nighttime walk took on the solemn aspect of a wedding march. Both knew that from now on they'd cling to each other even harder, not as lovers, but as two creatures who'd been alone and at last, after a long time, had found someone to walk with.

They were hardly man and woman. They were two beings who needed each other.

Their legs weak, they reached the peaceful environs of Washington Square. He knew Kay was surprised, wondering if he wasn't leading her back to their starting point, the diner where they'd met, or perhaps to Jessie's house, which she'd pointed out to him the night before.

He smiled to himself a little bitterly. He was afraid, very afraid, of what he was about to do.

They hadn't said they loved each other. Were they both superstitious about that word? Ashamed of it?

Combe recognized his street, and the door he'd passed through two nights earlier as he was running away, at wits' end, from his neighbors' commotion.

Tonight he was more composed. He walked with his head up. He felt like he'd done something that mattered.

But then he wanted to stop, to turn around, to plunge back into their unreal vagabond life.

He pictured, like a haven, the sidewalk in front of the Lotus, the purple neon sign, the shabby night clerk. It was all so easy!

'Here,' he said at last, and he stopped in front of his stoop.

The moment was definitive, like opening the doors of a church, and she knew it.

She went into the little courtyard bravely and looked around without surprise.

'Funny,' she said, straining to sound lighthearted. 'We were neighbors, and yet it took all that time for us to meet.'

They went into the foyer. There were the mailboxes with the doorbells underneath and nameplates over most of them.

Combe's name wasn't there. He saw she'd noticed.

'Come on. There's no elevator.'

'It's only four floors,' she said. She must have examined the building closely.

She went up the stairs ahead of him. On the third floor she stepped aside to let him by.

The first door to the left was J.K.C.'s. The next was Combe's. But before going to it, he felt he had to stop. He needed to look at her for a long moment, to take her in his arms and to kiss her slowly, deeply, on the lips.

'Come on.'

The hallway was dim and smelled of poverty. The door was an ugly brown, and the walls were grimy with fingerprints. Slowly he took his key out of his pocket, and with a strained laugh, he said, 'The last time I went out, I forgot to turn off the light. I noticed it from the street but I didn't have the energy to go back upstairs.'

He pushed open the door. The tiny entry was cluttered with suitcases and clothing.

'Come in.'

He was afraid to look at her. His hands were shaking.

He didn't say a thing. Either he pulled her or he pushed her, he didn't know which, but in any case he'd brought her to his place. Ashamed, anxious, at last he had asked her to come into his life.

The still-lighted lamp greeted them. The room was quiet, and the quietness was almost spectral. He had thought it would look sordid, but it was tragic, that was all, full of the tragedy of loneliness and abandonment.

The unmade bed with a dent in the pillow shaped like his head; the rumpled sheets of his insomnia; the pajamas, the slippers, the limp clothes thrown over the chairs.

And, on the table, next to an open book, what was left of a cold supper, the dreary meal of a lonely man.

Suddenly he realized everything he'd escaped from. He stood in the entry, frozen, head bowed, afraid to move.

He didn't want to look. Still he saw her, and he knew that she, too, was measuring the depth of his solitude.

He had thought she would be shocked and resentful.

She was shocked, but not that much – shocked to find out that his solitude was even more hopeless than her own.

What she noticed first were the pictures of the children, a boy and a girl.

'You, too,' she whispered.

Everything happened desperately slowly. Every tenth of a second counted, the tiniest fractions of time during which so much of the past and so much of the future was in play.

Combe looked away from his children's faces. He saw them as unhappy blurs becoming ever more blurred, and he was ashamed. He wanted to say he was sorry, but he didn't know for what or to whom.

Slowly, Kay stubbed out her cigarette in an ashtray. She took off her fur coat and hat and stepped behind him to close the door, which he'd left open.

Then, touching him lightly on the collar, she said, 'Darling, take off your coat.'

She helped him take it off and immediately hung it in its place in the closet.

She turned to look at him again – human, very much at home. She smiled, and there was something secret, almost joyous in her smile. At last, wrapping her arms around him, she said, 'You see, I knew.'

4

They slept that night like two people stranded in a railway station or in a car broken down by the road. They slept in each other's arms and, for the first time, they didn't make love.

'Not tonight,' she had begged in a whisper.

He understood – at least he thought he understood. They were both exhausted, dazed, as if they had been on an immense journey.

Had they actually arrived somewhere? They had gone to bed without tidying up the room. And, like people who go on feeling the pitch and roll of a ship for a few days after they return from a cruise, they still seemed to be walking, walking endlessly in the great city.

For the first time they woke when other people do. Combe glanced up, and he saw Kay opening the door into the hallway. Perhaps the click of the lock had torn him from his sleep, and his first thought was an anxious one.

But no. He saw her from the back, her hair silky and tangled. She was wrapped in one of his dressing gowns, with the hem trailing on the ground behind her.

'What are you looking for?'

She wasn't startled. She turned casually enough toward the bed, and the best thing was that she didn't try to smile.

'The milk. Doesn't it come every morning?'

'I don't like milk.'

'Oh.'

Before she joined him, she stepped into the kitchenette. The kettle on the hot plate was singing.

'What do you have in the morning – tea or coffee?'

It moved him to hear her voice in this room where he'd never had a visitor. Just before, he had been a little upset that she hadn't come to kiss him. Now he understood that it was better that way, with her puttering around, opening closets, bringing him a navy blue silk dressing gown.

'You want this one?'

She was wearing a pair of men's bedroom slippers, with the heels dragging on the floor behind her.

'What do you usually eat for breakfast?'

He relaxed, at peace. 'That depends. Usually, when I'm hungry, I go to the drugstore.'

'I found some tea and a can of coffee. Since you're French, I took a chance and made coffee.'

'I'll go get bread and butter.'

He felt very young. He wanted to go out, but it wasn't like yesterday, when he'd left the Lotus and then stopped within a hundred yards.

Now she was here, in his apartment. He was usually fastidious about the way he looked, perhaps a bit too much so, yet he almost went out unshaven, in his slippers, the way people did in Montmartre or Montparnasse or in working-class neighborhoods.

There was a hint of spring in the fall morning. He surprised himself by humming in the shower while Kay made the bed and hummed along.

It was as if an enormous weight had been lifted from his shoulders, the weight of years that had bent his back without his even knowing.

'Aren't you going to kiss me?'

And she offered him her lips as he left. He paused for a moment on the landing. He turned, opening the door again.

'Kay!'

She was standing where she had been, still looking at him from her side of the door.

'What?'

'I'm happy.'

'Me, too. Go on . . .'

He wasn't going to think about it. It was too new. Even the street was too new, or rather, it was the same street, but full of new things he'd never noticed before.

The drugstore, for example, where he'd often eaten breakfast alone while reading the paper. Now he saw it surrounded by a haze of happy irony mixed with self-pity.

He stopped, touched by the sight of an organ-grinder on the sidewalk; it was the first one he'd seen in New York, he could swear, the first one he'd seen since he was a child.

At the Italian grocery, it was new buying for two instead of one. He ordered little things he had never bought before. He wanted to fill the refrigerator.

He took the bread, butter, milk, and eggs with him and had the rest delivered. On his way out he remembered something.

'Leave a quart of milk at my door every morning.'

From below, he saw Kay at the window, and she waved to him. She met him at the top of the stairs and took the bags.

'Damn! I forgot something.'

'What?'

'Flowers. Yesterday morning I was going to get some for the apartment.'

'But isn't it better this way?'

'Why?'

'Because . . .'

She groped for the words, serious and smiling at the same time, with none of the embarrassment they had felt earlier that morning.

'. . . well, this way it feels less new, doesn't it? It's like it's been longer.'

Then she added quickly, because otherwise it might have been too much, 'You know what I was looking at out the window? There's an old Jewish tailor across the street. Have you ever noticed him?'

He vaguely remembered seeing an old man sitting cross-legged on a table, who spent the whole day sewing. He had a long, dirty beard. His fingers were dirty from handling fabric.

'When I was living in Vienna with my mother . . . I told you she was a famous concert pianist? Yes . . . But before that, things were hard. When I was little, we were poor. We lived in a single room . . . Oh, not as nice as this, since there was no kitchen, no refrigerator, no bathroom. There wasn't even running water, and we had to wash in a sink at the end of the hallway – I can't tell you how cold it was in winter.

'What was I saying? Oh, yes . . . When I was sick and had to stay home from school, I used to look out the window all day, and right across the street was an old Jewish tailor who looked so much like that one that for a moment I thought he was the same man.'

Combe said lightly, 'Maybe he is.'

'Idiot! He'd be a hundred at least. But don't you think it's a funny coincidence? I'm going to be in a good mood all day.'

'You needed something to put you in a good mood?'

'No . . . But I feel like a little girl again. I even feel like making fun of you. I made fun of everyone, you know, when I was young.'

'What have I done for you to make fun of me?'

'Can I ask you something?'

'Go ahead.'

'Why are there at least eight dressing gowns in your closet? I know I probably shouldn't ask. But it's pretty unusual for a man –'

'For a man who has so many dressing gowns to live in a place like this, that's what you mean? There's a simple answer really. I'm an actor.'

Why was he embarrassed he'd said it, and why had he avoided her eyes? All day the two of them were circumspect. They sat at the table with the breakfast leftovers on it. The limit of their vision was the window across the street where the tailor with his rabbinical beard sat sewing.

It was the first time they weren't surrounded by a crowd, the first time, in a way, that they were really face-to-face, just the two of them, without a jukebox or whiskey to fuel their intimacy.

Kay wasn't wearing lipstick. Her face looked softer, and there was a touch of shyness or fear in it. The change was so striking that her eternal cigarette didn't quite fit.

'Are you disappointed?'

'That you're an actor? Why should I be disappointed?'

But she seemed sad. And he knew why without having to talk. They both knew.

If an actor his age was living in Greenwich Village like this . . .

'It's a lot more complicated than you think,' he sighed.

'I wasn't thinking anything, darling.'

'I was well-known in Paris. You could say I was famous.'

'I have to admit, I don't remember your last name. You told me once, that first night, remember? I was embarrassed and I didn't want to ask again.'

'François Combe. I used to play at the Théâtre de la Madeleine, at the Michodière, at the Gymnase. I've toured all over Europe and in South America. I've also starred in a number of movies. Only eight months ago, I was offered a contract –'

She forced herself not to show pity, not to wound him.

'It's not what you think,' he went on hastily. 'I could go back anytime I want.'

She poured him a fresh cup of coffee. Her gesture was so natural he was surprised. The unexpected intimacy seemed miraculous.

'It's very simple and very silly. I might as well tell you. Everyone in Paris knows about it, and it was all over the papers. My wife was an actress, too, a famous actress. Marie Clairois.'

'I know that name.'

She was sorry she'd said it, but it was too late. She recognized his wife's name but not his.

'She's not so much younger than I am,' he went on. 'She's past forty. We've been married seventeen years. Our oldest child will soon be sixteen.'

He said it without passion, glancing at the photographs on the wall. He stood up, started pacing the room, and continued.

'Last winter, my wife announced suddenly that she was leaving me for a young actor, just out of school, who had been engaged by the Comédie Française. He was twenty-one years old. It was night, at our house in Saint-Cloud. I had it built myself, because I've always liked houses. I have bourgeois tastes, you know.

'I had just come home from the theater. She arrived home after me. She joined me in my study, and while she was announcing her decision to me, calmly, gently, affectionately, even tenderly, I had no doubt the boy was waiting for her in the taxi.

'I'm telling you –'

He cleared his throat.

'I was stunned – so shocked that I asked her to think it over. Now I can see how ridiculous my response was. I said, "Go to bed, my dear. We'll talk this over tomorrow, once you've slept on it."

'And she said, "François, I'm leaving now. Don't you understand that?"

'What was there to understand? That it was so urgent it couldn't wait until morning?

'In fact, I didn't understand. I might today. But that night I lost my temper. I must have said some pretty awful things.

'But she kept saying, always calmly, always with that almost maternal gentleness, "I'm so sorry, so sorry, François, that you can't understand!"'

Silence surrounded them, a silence so fine it didn't upset or embarrass them. Combe lit his pipe – a gesture he'd used in several of his roles.

'I don't know if you've seen Marie onstage or in a movie. She still plays young women, and she gets away with it. She has a very sweet, soft face, a little sad, with big eyes that are so innocent, like a fawn looking helplessly and reproachfully at the bad man who's just shot it. That was the kind of role she played in real life, too. It was the role she was playing that night.

'All the papers wrote about it, some in veiled terms, while others included every detail. The boy left the Comédie Française to debut with my wife in a new play. The theater sued him for breach of contract.'

'And your children?'

'My son's in England. He'd been at Eton for two years and I thought it best for him to stay there. My daughter's living with my mother in the country, near Poitiers. I could have stayed. I did for two months.'

'You loved her?'

He looked at her without understanding. For the first time, all of a sudden, words meant different things to them.

'I was offered the lead in a big movie she was going to be in, too, and I knew she'd end up getting her lover a part in it as well. In our business, we were destined to be thrown together all the time, you see?

'For example. Since we lived in Saint-Cloud and drove home together at night, we'd often meet up at Fouquet's, in the Champs-Élysées.'

'I know the place.'

'Like most actors, I never used to eat before a performance, but I would have a pretty big supper afterward. I had my table at Fouquet's, and they always knew just what I wanted. Well, a few days after my wife left me, she turned up there, and she wasn't alone. She came to shake my hand so simply, so unself-consciously, that the two of us, I mean the three of us, seemed to be playing a scene in a comedy.'

'"Good evening, François."

'The boy held out his hand, too. He stammered, "Good evening, Monsieur Combe."

'They were expecting me, I realized, to invite them to my table. I was caught. I can still see it. Some fifty people were watching us, including a couple of reporters.

'Then I announced, without thinking about what it meant: "I think I'll be leaving Paris soon."

'"Where are you going?" my wife asked.

'"I've been offered a contract in Hollywood. Now that there's nothing to keep me here . . ."

'Was she being cynical, or thoughtless? No. I don't think she was ever cynical. She believed me. She knew that I'd had an offer from Hollywood four years earlier and had turned it down, partly because of her, since there was nothing in it for her, and partly because of the children, who were too young to be separated from their father.

'She said to me, "I'm very happy for you, François. I always knew everything would work out."

'So. I'd kept them standing in front of my table until that moment. I asked them to sit down, I still ask myself why.

'"What can I offer you?"

'"You know very well that I don't eat supper, François. I'll have some juice."

'"And you?"

'The fool thought he had to order the same thing, so he didn't order a drink, which was what he really needed.'

'"Two juices, please."

'And I kept eating, with the two of them sitting there.

'"Any news from Pierrot?" my wife asked, pulling her compact out of her bag. Pierrot is my son's nickname.

'"I had a letter three days ago. He's still very happy there."

'"That's good," my wife said.

'So you see, Kay –'

Why just then did she say: 'Couldn't you call me Katherine?'

He reached out for her fingers as he paced by, squeezing them.

'You see, Katherine, all through supper my wife sat there casting little glances at that young fool, as if to say, "See how easy it is? There's no reason to be frightened."'

'You still love her, don't you?'

He circled the room twice, frowning. He kept staring at the old Jewish tailor across the way, and then he stopped in front of her. He fell silent for an instant, as he did onstage before a particularly dramatic line. Steeling his expression and with the sunlight in his eyes, he said: 'No!'

He wanted no emotion. He himself didn't feel any. And Kay shouldn't, either – that was the most important thing. He began talking again immediately, quickly, in a sharp voice.

'I left and I came to the United States. A friend, one of our best directors, once told me, "You can always go to Hollywood. A man like you doesn't have to wait for a contract. Go over there. See So-and-so and So-and-so. Tell them I sent you."

'I went and I was welcomed with open arms. Everyone was very polite. Do you see? Very polite, but no one offered me a thing.

'"If we decide to make such-and-such a film and there's a part for you, we'll be in touch."

'Or, "Maybe in a few months, when we set the schedule for our next production . . ."

'And that's it, Kay. You can see how stupid it all is.'

'I asked you to call me Katherine.'

'Forgive me. I'll get used to it. Some of my best friends are in Hollywood. They were wonderful. Everyone wanted to help. But I was just a deadweight in their busy lives.

'I didn't want to bother them any more. I preferred to be in New York. Besides, you can sign a contract just as easily here as in California.

'At first I lived in a grand hotel on Park Avenue. Then in a more modest hotel. Later I found this room. And then I was all alone. I was all alone, and that's the whole story.

'Now you know why I have so many dressing gowns, so many suits, so many shoes.'

He pressed his forehead against the windowpane. His voice faltered toward the end. He knew she was going to come up to him slowly and silently.

He was waiting without moving for the touch of her hand on his shoulder. He kept staring across the street at the bearded tailor, who was smoking an enormous porcelain pipe.

She whispered, 'Are you still very unhappy?'

He shook his head, but he wasn't going to turn around.

'Are you sure you don't love her anymore?'

And he lost his temper. He turned now, eyes full of fury.

'You idiot! Don't you get it?'

Because she had to understand. It was too important, more important than anything in the world. If she couldn't understand, who would?

Always this compulsion to blame everything on whatever was handy, to blame it all on a woman.

He paced feverishly. He hated her so much he refused to look at her.

'Can't you see that doesn't matter? What matters is me! Me! Me!' He almost screamed. 'Me, all alone, if that's what you want to hear. Me, naked and all alone, living here, yes, for six months! If you don't see that, you . . . you . . .'

And he nearly shouted, 'You aren't worthy of being here!'

But he caught himself. He fell silent, furious, scowling, like a child after a temper tantrum.

He wondered what Kay was thinking, what expression she was wearing, but he refused to look, staring at anything but her, at the stains on his wall. He shoved his hands in his pockets.

Why wasn't she helping? Why couldn't she say the right thing? Did she think it all came down to stupid sentimentality, did she really think that his drama was just the vulgar drama of someone whose wife had cheated on him?

He hated her. He detested her. Yes, he detested her. He tilted his chin to the left. When he was small, his mother used to say she could tell when he was up to no good because he cocked his head to the left.

He stole a glance. And he saw that she was smiling and crying at the same time. In her face, where he could make out the tracks of two tears, he read such joy and tenderness that he didn't know what to do. He didn't know how to look.

'Come here, François.'

Calling him that – she was too smart not to realize how dangerous that was right now. Was she so sure of herself?

'Come here.'

She spoke to him like a stubborn child.

'Come on.'

Reluctantly, he obeyed.

She should have been ridiculous, in her dressing gown that swept the floor and those big men's slippers, without makeup, her hair in a mess.

But she wasn't, and he moved toward her, still looking surly.

'Come.'

She took his head in her hands. She pushed it against her shoulder, pressing his cheek to hers. She held it there, almost by force, as if to fill him, bit by bit, with her heat and her presence.

He kept one eye open. Inside was a block of anger he meant to keep intact.

'You weren't as alone as I was,' she said. She said it softly. He wouldn't have heard the words if her lips hadn't been by his ear.

He stiffened; she must have felt him stiffen. But she was sure of herself, sure at least that the admission of their loneliness would make them indispensable to each other from now on.

'I have to tell you something, too.'

It was only a whisper, and stranger still, a whisper in broad daylight, in a sunlit room with no soft music in the background, nothing to help you escape yourself. A whisper in front of a window framing a shabby old Jewish tailor.

'I know I'm going to hurt you, because you're jealous. I'm glad you're jealous. But I have to tell you anyhow. When we met . . .'

And she didn't say 'the day before yesterday,' for which he was grateful, because he didn't want to think about how short a time they'd known each other.

She said, 'When we met' – and she said it even more softly, so that what she was confiding to him now seemed to vibrate within his chest – 'I was so alone, so hopelessly alone, I was so low, and I knew that I'd never pull out of it again, so I decided to leave with the first man who showed up, no matter who he was.

'I love you, François.'

She said it just once. She couldn't have said it again, since they were holding each other so tightly they couldn't speak. Everything was tight, their throats, their chests – their hearts that seemed to have stopped beating.

What could they say after that? What could they do? They couldn't even make love. It would have spoiled everything.

Combe didn't dare extricate himself from the embrace – because of the emptiness that was sure to follow. It was Kay who let go, smiling.

'Look across the street,' she said. 'He saw us.'

Sunlight slanted into the room. Trembling, it played on one of the walls of the apartment, a few inches from a child's photograph.

'François, you have to go out.'

There was sun in the streets, sun over the city. She knew he had to find a foothold in reality again. He had to do it for himself, and for both of them.

'You're going to dress differently. Yes! I'll pick the things you'll wear.'

There was so much he wanted to tell her after she'd said what she had. Why wouldn't she let him? She was fussing around, as though this was her place, her home. She was humming. It was their song, and she started to sing it as never before, in a voice that was deep and light and serious all at once. It was no longer another silly song but instead, for an instant, the essence of all they had just been through.

She was rummaging through the wardrobe. 'No, sir. No gray today. Or beige, either. Beige doesn't look good on you, whatever you think. You're not dark enough or fair enough for it.'

And, laughing, she asked, 'But, what color is your hair? Can you believe I've never noticed? Your eyes, yes. Your eyes change with your moods. When you were playing the martyr just now – or trying to play the martyr – they were an ugly dark gray, like a heavy sea that makes you seasick. I was wondering if you'd be able to make it the last few yards, or if I'd have to come rescue you.

'So, François, you will do as you're told. Here! Navy blue. I think you'll look wonderful in navy blue.'

He wished she'd leave him alone, but he didn't have the energy to resist.

Once again the thought came, *She's not even pretty.*

He hated himself for not having said he loved her, too.

Wasn't he sure? He needed her. He was scared of losing her and being alone again. What she'd confessed to him a few moments before . . .

He was deeply grateful for that, and yet he resented her. He said to himself: *It could have been me or anybody else.*

Then, reluctant yet moved, he let her dress him as though he were a child.

He knew that she didn't want to have another serious discussion, or more revelations, that morning. He knew she was playing a role, the role of the wife, a difficult one to play if you aren't in love.

'I'll bet, Mr Frenchman, you always wear a bow tie with this suit. To make you look even more French, I'm going to choose a blue one with polka dots.'

She was so right that he had to smile. He couldn't help it. At first he resisted. He was afraid of looking ridiculous.

'Plus a white handkerchief for your breast pocket. A little rumpled so you won't look like a mannequin in a store window. Where are your handkerchiefs?'

It was silly. Idiotic. They laughed, both playing their parts, trying to hide the tears in their eyes so they wouldn't be overcome with emotion.

'I'm sure there are people you have to see. Don't deny it. Don't lie. I insist you go see them.'

'Well, there's the studio,' he began.

'Good. Then you're going to the studio. Come back whenever you want. I'll be here.'

She knew he was frightened. She was so sure of it that words weren't enough to persuade him of her promise. She held him in her arms.

'Go on, François, *hinaus!*' It was a word from the first language she'd ever spoken. 'Off you go. And don't expect to find a big lunch when you come home.'

They were both thinking of Fouquet's, but they hid the thought.

'Take an overcoat. This one . . . and a black hat. Yes!'

She pushed him toward the door. She hadn't had time to wash her face or comb her hair.

He knew she wanted to be alone, and he wasn't sure if he was angry or grateful.

'I'll give you two hours. All right, three.' And she closed the door behind him.

But she opened it again immediately, pale and embarrassed. 'François!'

He came back up a few steps.

'I'm sorry I have to ask. But could you give me a few dollars – for lunch?'

He hadn't thought of it, and he blushed. He hadn't expected this . . . in the hallway, by the banister, across from the door with the letters J.K.C. painted in green.

He'd never felt more embarrassed in his life. He took his wallet out and hunted for the bills – he didn't want to look like he was counting them, it didn't matter to him – and blushed again, handing her some ones, twos, fives, he didn't want to know.

'I'm sorry.'

He knew. Of course. And it made his throat tighten. He wanted to go back into the apartment and tell her everything he was feeling. But he didn't dare, because of this question of the money.

'Do you mind if I buy a pair of stockings?'

Then he understood, or thought he did – she'd asked in order to restore his self-confidence, to make him feel like a man again.

'I'm sorry I didn't think of it before.'

'You know, I may get my things back.'

Now she was smiling. It had to be done with a smile, like their smile that morning.

'Go on. I'm not going to blow it all at the track.'

He looked at her. She still wasn't wearing makeup, still had no idea how she looked in the too-long dressing gown and the slippers that kept falling off her feet.

He stood a few steps below her.

He came back up.

That was their first real kiss of the day, their first real kiss ever perhaps, and it happened there, in the hallway, in a sort of no-man's-land, in front of anonymous doors. They were both so conscious of all it implied that they went on, dragged it out, sweetly, tenderly, not wanting it to end. Only the sound of a door shutting made their lips part.

'Go,' she said.

And feeling like a new man, he went.

5

Laugier, a French playwright who'd been in New York for two years, had helped him get radio work. And he'd played a Frenchman in a comedy on Broadway, but the show, which they'd staged in Boston first, had only run for three weeks.

He wasn't bitter that morning. He walked to Washington Square and took the Fifth Avenue bus. He stood on the platform, enjoying the spectacle of the street, and for a while he felt good.

The avenue was sunlit. The gray stones of the buildings had a golden hue, so that they seemed at times almost transparent, and the sky high above was all blue except for the occasional fluffy cloud like the ones around saints in religious paintings.

The radio studio was on Sixty-sixth Street, and when he got off the bus he still thought he was happy. But he felt vaguely uneasy, felt a trace of anxiety, a lack of balance that was almost a sense of foreboding.

What was he afraid of?

The thought crossed his mind that Kay might not be there when he got back. He shrugged. He was early for his appointment, so he stood at the window of an art gallery and watched himself shrug.

Why did his mood become darker the farther he got from Greenwich Village? He entered the building, took an elevator to the twelfth floor, and walked down the familiar hallway. At the end was a large, well-lit space with dozens of men and women sitting at work. In a cubicle he found the director of dramatic programming, a redheaded man with a face scarred by smallpox.

This was Hourvitch. Combe was struck by the fact that Hourvitch was Hungarian. He was struck by anything that reminded him of Kay.

'I was expecting a call from you yesterday, but it doesn't matter. Have a seat. You're on for Wednesday. By the way, your friend Laugier will be here in a few minutes. We'll probably be putting his new play on the air soon.'

Barely half an hour had passed since Kay had picked out his suit and practically dressed him, choosing his tie. At the time he had thought that it was one those unforgettable moments that bind people together forever, and now it seemed far away and unreal.

The director answered his telephone, and Combe let his gaze wander around the vast white room until it fastened on a big clock rimmed in black. He was trying to summon up the image of Kay's face, but couldn't.

It was her fault. He could almost see what she looked like when she was outside, in the street. He could almost see her again the way she'd been that first night, with her little black hat perched over her eyes, the lipstick staining her cigarette, her fur hanging down from her shoulders, but he was annoyed – no, worried – not to be able to picture her in any other way.

His impatience and nervousness must have shown, because the Hungarian asked, ear to the receiver, 'You in a hurry? You're not going to wait for Laugier?'

Yes, he was going to wait. But something had snapped inside, and his calm had left him – he didn't know when – taking with it his self-confidence and the happiness that was so new he hesitated to show it in public.

He looked guilty. When Hourvitch finally hung up the phone, Combe said with forced nonchalance, 'You're Hungarian – you must know Count Larski.'

'The ambassador?'

'I suppose. Yes, he must be an ambassador by now.'

'If he's the one I'm thinking of, he's impressive. Right now he's the Hungarian ambassador to Mexico. He'd been the first secretary at the embassy in Paris for a long time when I knew him. I guess you know I worked with Gaumont in Paris for eight years. Larski's wife, if I remember correctly, ran off with a gigolo . . .'

He had expected it. He felt ashamed. He had asked for it – those were the very words he had been waiting to hear – but now he wanted it to stop.

'That's all I need to know.'

But Hourvitch went on. 'I don't know what happened to her later. I ran into her once in Cannes when I was down there working on a film. I think I saw her in New York once.' He smiled and added, 'You know, in New York, you run into everybody these days, high, low. I think she must have been on the low side . . . Anyway, about your broadcast, what I wanted to tell you was . . .'

75

Was Combe still listening? He was sorry he'd come, sorry he'd ever opened his mouth. He felt like he'd dirtied something, but it was Kay he blamed.

He didn't know for what. Maybe, deep down, it was because she hadn't lied about everything.

Had he really believed she'd been the wife of a first secretary at an embassy? He didn't know now, but he was filled with anger. He thought bitterly, *When I get home, she'll be gone. Isn't leaving what she always does?*

The idea of the emptiness waiting to greet him was so intolerable that it caused him physical pain, a sharp pain in his chest. He wanted to leap in a taxi and go straight to Greenwich Village.

But, almost at the same time, he thought, *No. Of course she'll be there. Didn't she say that, on the night we met, if I hadn't come along, it could have been anybody?*

A cheery voice broke in: 'Well, old man, how are you?'

And he smiled. The fake grin must have made him look like an idiot because Laugier, who had just shown up, seemed troubled as he shook his hand.

'Is everything all right?'

'Yes, fine. Why?'

Laugier didn't let much bother him. Or if he did, he never showed it. He wouldn't say how old he was, but he had to be at least fifty-five. He had never been married. He lived surrounded by pretty girls, none older than twenty-five, and they changed constantly. He was like a juggler who could keep half a dozen pins in the air at once, without any of them ever seeming to touch his hands. The girls always disappeared without leaving a trace or causing any complication in Laugier's bachelor existence.

He was full of himself. When he invited you to dinner, he'd say, 'You're on your own? I have a charming friend here, and I'll ask her to bring along one of her little playmates.'

Was Kay still at the apartment? If only he could picture her face – just for a second. Again he tried and failed. He thought superstitiously: *It's because she isn't there.*

Then, perhaps because of Laugier and his good-natured cynicism, he buried the thought. He said to himself, *Of course she's there. If it worked before, it'll work again. Tonight she'll have a whole new show to put on for me.*

She was lying, that was certain. She had lied to him again and again. She even said as much. But how could he ever be sure that she was telling the truth? And he was suspicious of everything, even the story of the Jewish tailor and the sink at the end of the hall in Vienna, which had melted his heart.

'You look pale, old man. Come on, let's get a hamburger. I insist. It's on me. I'll be through with Hourvitch in three minutes.'

While the two men were talking business, why did he find himself thinking about his wife as well as about Kay?

Probably because of what the Hungarian had said: 'She ran off with a gigolo.'

People must have said the same thing about his wife. He didn't care. He had been honest that morning when he said he didn't love her anymore. And it wasn't even because of her that he had fallen to pieces. The truth was a lot more complicated.

Kay would never understand. Why should she? What sort of ridiculous pedestal had he placed her on just because he had run into her one night when he could no longer bear to be alone, a night when she was just looking for a man, or at least a bed?

Because it was a bed, all things considered, that she'd been looking for that night.

'Ready, old man?'

He sprang up, smiling agreeably.

'You should keep him in mind, Hourvitch, when you cast the part of the senator.'

A minor role, no doubt. Still it was good of Laugier. In Paris the situation would have been reversed. Seven years ago, at Fouquet's, in fact, Laugier, dead drunk, had insisted at three in the morning, 'Imagine, kiddo . . . the role of a lifetime . . . Three hundred performances, guaranteed, not to mention the road shows . . . But only if you're the lead, because without you there's no play . . . Do it! I've told you all about it . . . Now read the script, get cracking . . . If you go to the director of the Madeleine and tell him you want to do it, it's in the bag . . . I'll call you at six tomorrow . . . Don't you agree, my dear, he should star in my play?'

Because his wife had been with him that night. Laugier had slipped her the script with a conspiratorial smile, and the next day sent her a fabulous box of chocolates.

'Coming down?'

They left. He waited for the elevator and slipped behind his friend, always with an absent air.

'You see, old bean, New York's like that. One day you're . . .'

Combe wanted to beg him, 'Shut up, will you? Shut up, for God's sake!'

He knew the litany by heart. He'd heard it many times before. New York wasn't the point, he wasn't thinking about it anymore. He'd think about it later.

Only one thing mattered, that there was a woman at his place, in his room, a woman he knew nothing about, a woman who filled him with suspicion, a woman he could observe with eyes as clear and cold as he had ever looked at anyone with, a woman he loathed but couldn't do without.

'Hourvitch is a good fellow. A bit of a mixed bag, of course. He hasn't forgotten that he started out with a mop in his hand at the Billancourt studios, and he has scores to settle. Aside from that, he's okay, especially if you don't need anything from him.'

Combe was on the point of stopping short, shaking his friend's hand, and saying simply, 'Good-bye.'

People talk about the living dead. Possibly he had, too – like anybody else. Today, right now, on the corner of Sixty-sixth Street and Madison Avenue, he really was one of the living dead. His thoughts, his life, were somewhere else.

'You shouldn't take it so hard. A month from now, a month and a half, you'll be the first to laugh about the state you're in. You've got to be brave, if only to show those bastards who want to kick you when you're down. Why, I remember after my second play opened at the Porte-Saint-Martin . . .'

Why had she allowed him to go? She always guessed everything, so she must have known it wasn't the right moment yet. Unless she needed the freedom herself.

Was even the story about Jessie true? Those trunks locked up in an apartment with the key now slowly sailing to Panama . . .

'What'll you have?'

Laugier had steered him into a place not unlike their little place. There was the same jukebox by the counter.

'A manhattan.'

His fingers fished for a nickel in his pocket. He looked at himself in the mirror behind the shelf of glasses, and he cut such a ridiculous figure that he smiled sarcastically.

'What are you doing after lunch?'

'I have to go back.'

'Back where? I would have taken you to a rehearsal.'

The word reminded Combe of the rehearsals he'd been to in New York, in a tiny studio twenty or twenty-five stories above Broadway. The room was rented for the minimum amount of time possible, maybe an hour or two, he forgot. They'd still be hard at it when people from another cast showed up and crowded into the wings, waiting their turn.

It seemed that people knew only their own lines, their own part. They weren't aware of or interested in anything else. Especially not the other actors. No one said hello or good-bye.

Did anyone know his name? Maybe the ones he'd tried out with before. The director signaled to him. He came on, said his lines, and the only indication of human interest there'd been was the others laughing at his accent.

And he was frightened, terrified, at the thought of that loneliness, of going back to it, of standing between those painted canvas stage flats, where the loneliness was deeper than anywhere, even than in his room, even when, behind the thin walls, Winnie whoever-she-was and J.K.C. let themselves go on Friday night.

He was scarcely aware of walking to the jukebox, looking for a song, taking a nickel out of his pocket, putting it in the slot.

The song had just started when Laugier, nodding to the bartender to refill their glasses, said: 'Do you know how much that song has earned in the United States alone? A hundred thousand dollars in royalties, old man, for both the music and lyrics, of course. And it's just starting to make its way around the rest of the world. Right now there are two thousand jukeboxes just like that one playing it, not to mention bands, the radio, restaurants. Sometimes I wonder if I shouldn't write songs instead of plays. Cheers. You want to grab a bite?'

'Would you mind if I didn't?'

He looked so serious when he replied that Laugier stared at him, surprised and, in spite of his usual irony, somehow awed.

'You really are in bad shape, aren't you?'

'I'm sorry . . .'

'Of course, old . . . Listen . . .'

No. It was impossible. His nerves were on edge. Even the street, with its racket he usually didn't notice, its stupid hustle-bustle, was maddening. He stood for a minute or two at the bus stand, and then, when a taxi stopped nearby, he ran over, jumped inside, and gave his address.

He wasn't sure what he feared most, finding her there or not finding her there. He was mad at himself, and at Kay, without knowing exactly why. He felt humiliated, terribly humiliated.

The streets flashed by. He didn't look at them or recognize them. He thought to himself, *She grabbed her chance and ran, the bitch.*

At almost the same time, he thought: *Me or somebody else . . . It doesn't matter who . . . Or the gigolo in Cannes . . .*

Through the window he looked up and down his street as if expecting it to have changed somehow. He was pale and knew it. His hands were clammy, and his forehead was damp.

She wasn't at the window. He didn't see her there, as he had in the morning, when the sun was shining and the day was new and she slid her hand gently, lovingly against the glass.

He ran up the stairs and didn't stop until the third floor. He was so furious that he was ashamed. For a moment, he could have laughed.

There, against the slightly sticky banister, that morning, just two hours earlier . . .

He couldn't wait any longer. He had to know if she was gone. He jammed his key into the lock and was still fumbling when the door swung back.

Kay was there, smiling at him.

'Come on,' he said, not looking at her.

'What's the matter?'

'Nothing. Come on.'

She was wearing her black silk dress. Obviously she had nothing else to wear. But she must have bought the little white embroidered collar. He didn't recognize it, and it infuriated him.

'Come on.'

'But lunch is ready.'

He could see. He could see perfectly well that the room had been all tidied up, which it hadn't been for a long time. He could also imagine the bearded tailor across the street, but he didn't want to think about him.

He didn't want to think about anything. Not Kay, who was bewildered, even more bewildered than Laugier had been just now. But in her eyes, too, he saw the same submission and respect.

He was at the end of his rope. Didn't they realize that? If they didn't, let them say so. He'd crawl off to die in a corner, all alone.

There!

As long as they didn't make him wait, as long as they didn't ask him any questions. Because he'd had enough of questions. The ones he asked himself, in any case, the ones that were turning him into a nervous wreck.

'Well?'

'I'm coming, François. I thought . . .'

Thought what! Thought she'd fix him a nice lunch – he could see, he wasn't blind. And then? Was that how he loved her, with her blissful air of a new bride? Were the two of them already able to just stop?

Not him, at any rate.

'But the hot plate . . .'

To hell with the hot plate, which could burn away until someone had time to think about him. Hadn't the light been on, too, for forty-eight hours? Had he worried about that?

'Come on.'

What was he so afraid of? Kay? Himself? Fate? All he knew for sure was that he needed them to plunge back into the crowd, to walk, to stop at little bars, to rub up against strangers, people you didn't have to apologize to for bumping into them or stepping on their toes, maybe he even needed Kay to drive him up the wall, leaving a smudge of lipstick on the tip of her so-called last cigarette.

Did she really understand?

They were on the sidewalk. He had no idea where to go anymore, and she wasn't curious enough to ask.

She took his arm. 'Come on,' he dully repeated, as if accepting once and for all whatever fate held in store.

The hours that followed were exhausting. He seemed almost sadistically determined to revisit all the places they'd been together.

At the Rockefeller Center cafeteria, for example, he ordered exactly what they'd had the first time. Scrutinizing her fiercely, he subjected her to a merciless interrogation.

'Who have you been here with before?'

'What do you mean?'

'Don't ask questions. Answer me. When a woman answers a question with a question, she's about to tell a lie.'

'I don't understand, François.'

'You told me you came here often. Admit it would be unusual if you always came alone.'

'Sometimes I came with Jessie.'

'Who else?'

'I don't remember.'

'With a man?'

'Possibly, yes, a long time ago, with a friend of Jessie's . . .'

'A friend of Jessie's who was also your lover.'

'But . . .'

'Admit it.'

'I mean . . . Yes, I think . . . Once, in a taxi.'

And he saw the inside of the cab, the driver's shoulders, the milky blur of faces crowded in the darkness outside. He could feel those stolen kisses on his lips, he could taste them.

'Bitch!'

'It was so meaningless, Frank . . .'

Why was she calling him Frank all of a sudden?

It was him or anybody else, right? One man more or one man less?

Why didn't she fight back? He resented her passivity, her humility. He dragged her outside. He kept dragging her around everywhere, as if driven to it by some obscure force.

'And this street, have you been here with a man?'

'No. I don't know anymore.'

'New York is so big, isn't it? Still, you've lived here for years. You don't expect me to believe that you haven't gone to little bars like ours with other men, and that you haven't endlessly played other records that were at that moment *your* song.'

'I've never been in love, Frank.'

'You're lying.'

'Think what you like. I've never been in love. Not the way I love you.'

'And you went to the movies. I know you've been at the movies with a man and done things in the dark. Admit it!'

'I don't know anymore.'

'See! Was it on Broadway? Show me the cinema.'

'Maybe at the Capitol, once . . .'

They were less than a hundred yards away from it and saw the red-and-yellow letters blinking on and off.

'A young naval officer. A Frenchman.'

'You were lovers a long time?'

'A weekend. His ship was in Boston. He came to New York on leave with a friend.'

'And you had both of them!'

'When his friend saw how things were going, he left us.'

'I'll bet you met them on the street.'

'That's true. I recognized the uniform. I heard them speaking French. They didn't know I understood them until I smiled. They spoke to me.'

'Which hotel did he take you to? Where did you sleep with him? Answer me!'

She remained silent.

'Answer me!'

'Why do you want to know? You're torturing yourself for nothing, believe me. It was so unimportant, Frank.'

'Which hotel?'

As if resigned to fate, she said: 'The Lotus.'

He burst out laughing and dropped her arm.

'Oh, God, that takes the prize! Talk about coincidences! So, on our first night, or first morning, rather, since it was nearly day, when I brought you to the –'

'François!'

'Yes. You're right. I'm being stupid, aren't I? As you say, it's so unimportant.'

Then, after a few steps: 'I'll bet he was married, your officer, that he talked to you about his wife.'

'And he showed me pictures of his children.'

Staring straight ahead, he saw the pictures of his own children on his wall, and still he dragged her on. They reached their little bar. He shoved her inside.

'You're sure, absolutely sure, that you haven't come here before with someone else? You'd better admit it now.'

'I've never been here with anyone but you.'

'Maybe, after all, for once you're telling the truth.'

She wasn't resentful. She was doing her best not to be upset. She held out her hand for a nickel. She didn't protest. As if performing a rite, she went to put on their record.

'Two scotches.'

He drank three or four. He pictured her in other bars with other men, dragging out the night, begging for a last drink, lighting a last cigarette, always the last. He pictured her waiting on the sidewalk for the man, walking awkwardly because her heels were too high and her feet hurt, taking his arm . . .

'Don't you want to go home?'

'No.'

He wasn't listening to the music. He seemed to be looking inside himself. Suddenly he paid the bill. Once again, he said: 'Come on.'

'Where are we going?'

'To look for other memories. Which is to say we could go pretty much anywhere, couldn't we?'

The sight of a dance hall made him ask, 'Do you dance?' She misunderstood. She said, 'Do you want to go dancing?'

'I only asked you if you dance.'

'Yes, François.'

'Where did you go those nights when you felt like dancing? Show me. Don't you understand that I want to know? And listen. If we run into a man . . . Are you listening to me? A man you've slept with. It's bound to happen one of these days, if it hasn't already. When it happens, I want you to do me a favor, tell me, "That one."'

Without meaning to, he turned back toward her, noting that her face was flushed and her eyes glistening. But he didn't feel sorry for her, he was too unhappy for that.

'Tell me. Have we come across one?'

'Of course not.'

She was crying. She cried without crying, like a child hanging on to its mother's hand while being dragged through a crowd.

'Taxi!'

He shoved her in. 'This should stir some memories,' he said. 'Who was he, this taxicab lover of yours? Assuming there was just the one. It's quite the thing in New York, isn't it, sex in a taxi? Who was he?'

'I already told you, a friend of Jessie's. Of her husband, Ronald, I mean. We met him by accident.'

'Where?'

He needed to fix the images in his mind.

'In a little French restaurant on Forty-second Street.'

'And he bought you champagne. And then Jessie discreetly withdrew, like your sailor's friend. How discreet people can be! They understand right away. Let's get out here.'

It was the first time they had come back to the corner and the diner where they'd met.

'What do you want to do?'

'Nothing. Just a pilgrimage. And here?'

'What do you mean?'

'You know very well what I mean. It couldn't have been the first time you came here to eat at night. It's right near where you lived with your Jessie. I'm beginning to know both of you, and I'd be amazed if you hadn't struck up a conversation with someone. You have quite a knack for engaging men in conversation, don't you, Kay?'

He looked at her face, and it was drawn. He looked so hard that she didn't have the courage to reply. He tightened his grip on her arm, his fingers cruel as pincers.

'Come on.'

Night had fallen. They passed Jessie's building, and Kay stopped short, surprised to see a light on inside.

'François, look!'

'So what? Your girlfriend's back home? Unless it's Enrico. You'd like to go up, wouldn't you? Say it! You'd like to go up?' His voice was threatening. 'What are you waiting for? Are you scared I'll go up with you and discover all the little secrets hidden away up there?'

But this time it was she who said, tearfully, 'Come on.'

They walked on, once again along Fifth Avenue, heads down, in silence, blind to everything but the trouble and bitterness between them.

'I'm going to ask you a question, Kay.'

He seemed calmer, almost in control of himself. She whispered, waiting, even feeling a little hope, 'I'm listening.'

'Promise me you'll answer honestly.'

'Of course.'

'Promise.'

'I swear.'

'How many men have there been your life?'

'What do you mean?'

Aggressive again, he pressed, 'You didn't understand me?'

'It depends on what you mean by being in a woman's life.'

'How many men have you slept with?' He prompted her sardonically, 'A hundred? A hundred and fifty? More?'

'A lot less.'

'Which means?'

'I don't know. Wait . . .'

She was searching her memory. Her lips moved as though she were reciting names or figures.

'Seventeen. No, eighteen . . .'

'You're sure you're not forgetting anyone?'

'I don't think so. Yes, that's all of them.'

'Including your husband?'

'Sorry. I didn't count him. That makes nineteen, darling. But if only you knew how unimportant it is . . .'

'Come on.'

They turned around. They were exhausted, heads and bodies empty. They said nothing – they didn't even try to think of things to say.

Washington Square . . . the deserted side streets of Greenwich Village . . . the basement-level laundry where the Chinese man ironed under a harsh light . . . the red-checked curtains of the Italian restaurant.

'Go on up.'

He walked behind her. He seemed so composed and so cold that she felt a shiver on the back of her neck. He opened the door.

He almost sounded like a judge: 'You can go to bed.'

'And you?'

Him? What, in fact, was he going to do? He slid behind the curtain and pressed his forehead against the window-pane. He heard her moving around the room. He heard the sound of the bedsprings as she got into bed, but he stayed by the window for a long time wrapped in his solitude.

Finally he came to her, studied her, his face motionless. He whispered, 'You . . .'

And he repeated it, more and more loudly, until he was shouting at her in despair: 'You! . . . You! . . . You! . . .'

His fist hung in space, and perhaps in another moment he might have controlled it.

'You! . . .'

His voice was hoarse. And he hit her in the face as hard as he could with his fist, once, twice, three times . . .

At last, completely spent, he collapsed on her, sobbing and begging for forgiveness.

Her voice was far away, and they could taste the salt of their tears on their lips, when she said, 'My poor darling.'

6

They woke up very early though they didn't realize it. They thought they must have slept for an eternity. Neither of them bothered to look at the clock.

Kay got up first to open the curtains, and she cried, 'Look, François!'

For the first time since he'd lived here, he saw that the Jewish tailor wasn't sitting cross-legged on his table. He was sitting in a chair like anyone else, an old straw-bottomed chair he must have brought with him from the far reaches of Poland or the Ukraine. With his elbows on the table, he was dipping thick slices of bread into a flowered porcelain bowl and looking placidly in front of him.

Over his head, the electric bulb, which at night he pulled over to his work area with a metal wire, was still on.

He was eating slowly, studiously, and in front of his eyes was nothing but a wall hung with scissors and patterns on thick gray paper.

Kay said, 'He's my friend. I have to find some way to make him happy.'

Because they both felt happy.

'Do you realize it's not even seven yet?'

Neither felt at all tired. They felt nothing but an immense and profound sense of well-being, which made them smile, from time to time, at the most trivial things.

Watching her put on her clothes while he poured boiling water over the coffee, he thought out loud, 'There must have been somebody in your friend's apartment last night, since the light was on.'

'I'd be very surprised if Jessie had been able to come back.'

'You'd like to get your clothes, wouldn't you?'

She still didn't dare accept what she sensed was generosity.

'Listen,' he went on. 'I'll go back there with you. I'll wait downstairs while you go up.'

'You think?'

He knew what was on her mind, that she might run into Enrico or even Ronald, Jessie's husband. 'Let's go.'

And they went. It was so early in the morning that the street seemed different, unknown. No doubt they'd both been out that early before, but it was the first time they'd done it together. After their night wanderings along sidewalks and through bars, they felt washed clean by the morning freshness, with the messy city sprucing itself up for the new day.

'Look. There's a window open. Go on up. I'll wait here.'

'I'd rather you came with me, François. You don't mind, do you?'

They climbed the stairway, which was clean, unostentatious, very proper. There were doormats in front of nearly every apartment, and on the second floor a cleaning lady polished a brass doorknob so energetically it made her ample breasts quiver.

He knew Kay was a little frightened. She must have thought it was some kind of test. Yet everything seemed obvious to him, the building ordinary, sober, unmysterious.

She rang the bell, and her lips trembled as she glanced his way, squeezing his hand for reassurance.

No one answered the bell, which echoed in the emptiness inside.

'What time is it?'

'Nine.'

'Do you mind?'

She rang the bell of the next apartment. A man of about sixty in a quilted dressing gown, his scant gray hair forming a crown around his pink scalp, answered the door, a book in his hand. He bowed his head to peer over the rims of his glasses.

'Well! It's you, my little miss. I thought you'd come by sooner or later. Was Mr Enrico able to reach you? He stopped by last night. He asked me if you'd left your new address. I take it you have some personal effects in the apartment he wishes to return.'

'Thank you, Mr Bruce. I'm sorry to bother you. I wanted to be sure it was Mr Enrico who had come back.'

'No news of your friend?'

How banal and familiar it all was!

When they were in the street again, she said, 'I don't know why Enrico has a key. Or, actually, I think I do. At first, you see, when Jessie's husband got the job in Panama and she realized the climate didn't agree with her, she moved to a place in the Bronx. At the time she was working as a receptionist in a building on Madison Avenue. Once she met Enrico and made up her mind – because, whatever you may think, it was five months before anything happened between them – he insisted she come live here. He just paid the rent, you see? I don't know how they worked it out, but I wonder now if he hadn't rented the apartment in his name.'

'Why don't you phone him?'

'Who?'

'Enrico, my sweet. Since he has a key to the apartment and all your things are there, what could be more natural?'

He wanted it to seem quite natural. And it did, this morning.

'You really want me to?'

He squeezed her hand. 'Please.'

He led her by the arm to the nearest drugstore. Only there did she remember that Jessie's lover never got to work before ten o'clock, so they waited quietly, so quietly that they could have been mistaken for a long-married couple.

Twice she returned unsuccessfully from the phone booth. The third time, he saw through the glass that she had made contact with her past again on the other end of the line, though she didn't take her eyes off him. She was smiling at him shyly and gratefully and asking for his forgiveness at the same time.

'He's coming. Do you mind? There was nothing else to do. He said he'd hop in a taxi and be here in ten minutes. He couldn't say much because there was somebody in his office. All I know is he got the key by messenger, in an envelope with Ronald's name on it.'

He wondered if she'd take his arm while they were waiting on the sidewalk for the South American, and she did, without a hint of strain. A taxi soon pulled up. She looked into his eyes again, as if making a promise, and her own eyes were very clear – she held his gaze so he could see how clear – while the pout on her lips asked him to be brave, or else indulgent.

He didn't need to be either. He felt so easy now that he had a hard time keeping a straight face.

This Enrico, this Ric around whom he had created such a world, was a little man of no particular consequence. Not bad-looking, true. But so average, so unprepossessing! He felt obliged, under the circumstances, to rush theatrically up to Kay, effusively clasping her hands.

'My poor Kay! That this should happen to us!'

Very simply, she introduced him: 'My friend François Combe. You can talk freely, since he knows everything.'

Combe noted that she used the familiar *tu* with Enrico.

'Let's go on up. I have a meeting in fifteen minutes. I'll tell the cab to wait.'

Enrico went up the stairs first. He was a small man, perfectly groomed. A cloud of cologne trailed behind him. Combe could tell that he had curled his dark, pomaded hair.

Enrico rooted around for the key in his pocket, which was filled with them. Combe noted it with pleasure, since he hated men who carried too many keys. Finally Enrico found the one he was looking for – found it in a jacket pocket – after a long search during which his feet in their delicate leather shoes tapped feverishly on the floorboards.

'I was completely *devastated* when I came here and found nobody! Luckily I thought of ringing the bell of the nice old gentleman next door, who gave me the note she'd left for me.'

'For me, too.'

'I know. He told me. I didn't know where to find you.'

He stole a glance at Combe, who grinned. Maybe Enrico was expecting some sort of an explanation from Kay, but all she gave him was a happy smile.

'Then yesterday I received the key, no note. I came in the evening.'

My God, how simple it all was! How utterly prosaic! The open window created a draft, and the door slammed shut behind them after they had slipped inside. It was an ordinary small apartment, like thousands of others in New York, with the same cozy nook in the living room, the same coffee table and side tables, the same ashtrays beside the armchairs, the same record player, the same tiny bookcase in a corner by the window.

It was here that Kay and Jessie . . .

Combe smiled without being aware of it, a smile that seemed to rise up out of his flesh. There may have been a trace of malice in his eyes, but not much of one, and he wondered, when the realization dawned, whether Kay was annoyed by it. What picture had he drawn of the life she had led here, of these men she tortured him with by always calling them by their first names?

One of them stood before him now, and he couldn't help noticing that at ten o'clock in the morning he was wearing a pearl pin on his multicolored tie.

After closing the window, Kay went into the bedroom.

'Can you give me a hand, François?'

She used the familiar *tu* again, and he knew it was out of kindness. It was nice of her to emphasize the intimacy they shared.

She opened a battered trunk and glanced into a wardrobe.

She said, surprised, 'Jessie didn't take any of her things!'

Enrico said, lighting a cigarette, 'I can explain. I had a letter from her this morning that she wrote from the *Santa Clara*.'

'She's already at sea?'

'He made her take the first boat back with him. It didn't turn out as badly as I thought. When he arrived, he knew exactly what was going on. I'll let you read the letter. She had a steward send it, since he won't let her out of his sight. He came here and said, "You're alone?"

'"As you can see for yourself."

'"He's not going to show up, is he?"'

Enrico went on, holding his cigarette in the arch manner of an American woman: 'You know Jessie. She didn't say so in her letter, but she must have argued, gotten angry, made a scene . . .'

Combe looked at Kay, and they both smiled.

'It seems Ronald was very cool.'

So! Enrico called him by his first name, too.

'I wonder if he didn't come to New York just for that, the moment he heard from whoever tipped him off. He went to the wardrobe while Jessie was screaming blue murder, took out my pajamas and dressing gown, and threw them on the bed.'

They were still there. A not quite brand-new floral-pattern dressing gown and cream-colored silk pajamas with a dark red monogram.

'While she was crying, he calmly went through her things. He only let her take what she had three years ago, when she came back from Panama. You know Jessie . . .'

It was the second time he'd used that little phrase. Combe, too, felt he was beginning to know Jessie. Not only Jessie but Kay, who'd become so understandable that he had to laugh at himself.

'You know Jessie. She just couldn't give up her dresses and things, and she said, "I swear, Ronald, I bought these myself."'

Did Enrico actually have a sense of humor?

'I wonder how she managed to write it all down in the letter. She says he doesn't leave her alone for a minute, that he's with her the whole time, watching what she does, looking at what she looks at, and yet she managed to write me six pages, some of them in pencil, telling me everything. There's a note to you, too, Kay. She said to take whatever she left, if you like.'

'Thank you, Enrico, but I couldn't.'

'The rent's paid until the end of the month. I don't know what I'll do with all my stuff here, since I can't really take them home. If you want me to leave you the key . . . Well, I will regardless, since I have to go now. I have a very important meeting this morning. I suppose that, now they're at sea, Ronald will calm down a little.'

'Poor Jessie!'

Did Enrico feel guilty? He said, 'I wonder what I could have done. I had no idea what was happening. That night my wife was having a dinner party, and I couldn't even telephone. Good-bye, Kay. Just send the key to my office.'

Enrico wasn't sure what to do about this man he scarcely knew, and he shook his hand with exaggerated warmth. Then he felt he had to say, almost as a mark of approval, 'She's Jessie's best friend.'

'What's the matter, François?'

'Nothing, darling.'

It was the first time he'd called her that without a hint of sarcasm.

Perhaps the realization that Enrico was so small made her seem smaller, too. He wasn't disappointed, though. In fact, he felt an almost infinite gratitude toward her.

Enrico was gone, leaving behind a faint whiff of cologne, his pajamas, his dressing gown on the bed, and a pair of slippers on the floor of the armoire.

'Now do you see?' Kay whispered.

'Yes, love, I see.'

It was true. It was good that he'd come, since he had seen her at last, her and her crowd, all those Enricos and

Ronalds, those sailors, those friends, all of them now shrunk down to their proper dimensions.

He didn't love her any less. He loved her more tenderly. With less strain, less anger, less bitterness. He had almost lost his fear of her and of the future. Perhaps, if he lost all his fear, he would surrender entirely.

'Sit down,' she said to him. 'You're crowding the place.'

Did the bedroom she'd shared with Jessie seem smaller to her, too? It was bright and pleasant. The walls were painted a soft white, the cretonne spreads on the twin beds were imitation toile de Jouy, and the drapes, made of the same fabric, let the sun filter in.

He sat down obediently on the bed, next to the flower-print dressing gown.

'I was right, wasn't I, not to want to take anything that belongs to Jessie? Look! Do you like this dress?'

It was a simple evening gown, quite pretty. She held it up in front of her like a salesgirl in a pricey shop.

'Have you worn it a lot?'

Would she take it the wrong way? No – and it wasn't jealousy this time. He'd said it pleasantly, because he was grateful to her for flirting with him so innocently.

'Just twice. And nobody so much as touched me either time. Nobody even kissed me.'

'I believe you.'

'Really?'

'I believe you.'

'Here are the shoes that go with it. The gold's a little too shiny for my taste. I wanted something more muted, but these were all I could afford. I'm not boring you, am I?'

'Absolutely not.'

'You sure?'

'Quite the opposite. Come give me a kiss.'

She hesitated, not for her sake, he knew, but out of an odd sort of respect. Then she leaned down and brushed his lips with hers.

'That's my bed you're sitting on, you know.'

'And Enrico?'

'He only spent a couple of nights a month here, sometimes less. Because of his wife, he had to pretend he was on business trips. And that was complicated, because she always wanted to know what hotel he was staying at, and she'd call him in the middle of the night.'

'She suspected something?'

'I think she did, but she pretended not to. She wasn't dumb. I don't think she ever loved him, or she'd stopped loving him but was still jealous. If she'd confronted him, he would have divorced her and married Jessie.'

That little man with the pearl pin on his tie? It was good to be able to listen to all this now, to be able to automatically assign the proper weight to words as well as things.

'He often came in the evening. Every two or three days. He had to leave around eleven, and those nights I usually went to a movie to give them some privacy. I'll show you the theater where I'd see the same movie two or three times because I didn't dare take the subway anywhere else.'

'Don't you want to put on that dress?'

'How did you know?'

She still held it in her hands. Quickly, with a movement he'd never seen her use before, she slipped out of her everyday black dress, and he felt as though he was looking at her in all her intimacy for the first time. Was it in fact the first time he'd seen her without clothes?

Strange: he hadn't been that curious about her body. They'd been together and bruised each other savagely, and only last night they'd fallen as if into an abyss, and yet still he couldn't have said what her body was like.

'Should I change slips, too?'

'Everything, darling.'

'Go lock the door.'

It was almost a game – and deeply pleasurable. This was the third room they'd been in together, and in each he'd discovered not only a new Kay but new reasons to love her, different ways of loving her.

He sat down on the edge of the bed again and watched her, naked, her skin very white with a trace of gold where the sunlight came in through the drapes. She was rummaging around in drawers of lingerie.

'I wonder what to do about my things at the dry cleaners. They'll bring it here, but no one will be home. We should probably stop by. Do you mind?'

She hadn't said, 'I should stop by'; she had said, 'We should stop by,' as though from now on they would never spend a second apart.

'Jessie has much prettier things than I do. Look at this.'

She rubbed the silk with her fingers, then held it out for him to feel.

'She has a much better figure, too. Do you want me to put this on? It's not too pink for your taste? Oh, I've got a black lace corset, too. I always wanted a corset, and I finally bought one. But I didn't feel like wearing it. It seemed too racy somehow.'

She brushed her hair. Her hand found the brush without her having to look for it. The mirror was exactly where it had to be. She held a pin in her mouth.

'Would you zip me up?'

That was the first time. What an amazing number of things they were doing for the first time that morning, including, for him, kissing her delicately on the neck, without greediness, breathing on the down on her nape, then sensibly sitting on the foot of the bed.

'Like the dress?'

'It's pretty.'

'I bought it on Fifty-second Street. It was very expensive, you know. At least it was for me.'

She gave him a pleading look.

'Do you want to go out together one night? I could wear this, and you could dress up . . .'

Without a transition, just when he least expected it, or maybe when she herself least expected it, great tears filled her eyes. Her smile hadn't yet had time to vanish from her face.

She turned her head away and said, 'You've never asked me what I do.'

She was still in her evening gown, her feet bare in the golden pumps.

'And I didn't want to talk about it because I was ashamed. I preferred, stupidly, to let you imagine things. There were times I did it on purpose.'

'Did what on purpose?'

'You know very well! When I knew Jessie, we were working in the same building. That's how we met. We used to eat lunch at the same drugstore. I'll show it to you, too – it's on the corner of Madison Avenue. Since I speak several languages, I was hired as a translator.

'Only there's something you don't know, something very silly. I told you a little about my life with my mother. When she began to get famous, I spent most of the time traveling with her, since she didn't want to leave me alone, and I pretty much stopped going to school.

'Whatever you do, don't laugh at me. There was one thing I never learned: how to spell. Larski used say, in a cold voice that still makes me feel ashamed, that I wrote like a scullery maid.

'Now do you understand? Unzip me, will you?'

She came over and offered him her back, white, milky, a bit bony where it showed between the half-open black dress.

When he caressed her, she begged: 'No, not just yet, okay? I'd like so much to talk a bit more.'

In just her panties and bra, she got out her cigarettes and lighter and sat cross-legged on Jessie's bed, an ashtray within reach.

'They transferred me to the mailroom. It was way in back, in a windowless room with no light, and three of us stuffed envelopes there all day long. The two other girls were cows. We had nothing to talk about. They hated me. We wore rough cotton aprons because of the glue. I did everything to keep mine clean. But I'm boring you. It's ridiculous, isn't it?'

'Not at all.'

'You're just saying that . . . Well, you asked for it. Every morning, I'd find my apron already glue-stained. They even put glue inside so it would get on my dress. Once I fought with one of them, a squat little Irish girl with a face like an Eskimo. She was stronger than me. She made sure she ruined the brand-new pair of stockings I had on.'

He said, with a tenderness that felt deep and light at the same time, 'My poor Kay.'

'You think I was acting like Mrs First Secretary at the Embassy? I absolutely wasn't, I swear it. If Jessie were here, she'd tell you.'

'I believe you, darling.'

'I admit I couldn't face staying there. Because of the two girls, you understand? I thought it would be easy to find another job. I was out of work for three weeks. That's when Jessie suggested I sleep at her place, because I couldn't pay my rent. She was living in the Bronx then, as I said, in a sort of huge barracks with iron fire escapes running up and down the brick front. The whole building smelled of cabbages, I don't know why. For months we lived with the taste of cabbage in our throats.'

'I finally found a job at a movie theater on Broadway. Remember when you were talking to me yesterday about theaters?'

Her eyes welled up again.

'I was an usherette. Doesn't sound like much, does it? I know I'm not particularly strong, since I spent two years in a sanatorium. But the others were no better off than me. At night we were all ready to drop. Other times, because of the endless bumping through crowds, hours and hours of it with that constant music and those loud, unreal voices coming out of the walls, our heads would start spinning.

'I've seen girls faint dozens of times. If they fainted in the theater itself, they were out of a job. Looks bad, you know . . .

'Am I boring you?'

'No. Come here.'

She edged closer, but they stayed on their separate beds. He lifted his hand and caressed her, surprised that her skin was so soft. Between her panties and her bra, he discovered alluring contours and shadows he'd never noticed before.

'I was very sick. Once, four months ago, I spent seven weeks in the hospital, and only Jessie came to see me. They wanted to send me to a sanatorium again, but I refused. Jessie begged me to stop working for a while. When you met me, I'd been job-hunting for about a week.'

She smiled defiantly.

'I'll find one, too.'

Then, abruptly, 'Wouldn't you like a drink? There must be a bottle of whiskey in the cupboard. Unless Ronald drank it, which would surprise me.'

She came back from the other room with a nearly empty bottle. She went to the refrigerator. He couldn't see her. He heard himself cry out, 'What's the matter?'

'You'll laugh. Ronald even thought to unplug the refrigerator. That wouldn't have crossed Enrico's mind yesterday. It's just like Ronald. You heard what Jessie wrote. He didn't get mad. He didn't say anything. He sorted out her things. And you'll notice that he didn't leave anything lying around, like someone else would have done in his place. When we got here everything was tidy; my dresses were where I'd left them. Everything put back except Enrico's dressing gown and pajamas. Don't you think that's funny?'

No. He didn't think anything. He was happy. It was a new kind of happiness. If, the day before, or even that morning, someone had said that he'd be lying around lazily, voluptuously, in this bedroom, he never would have believed it. He lay stretched out, a ray of sunlight shining on him, on this bed that had been Kay's, his hands clasped behind his head, letting his surroundings sink in, detail by detail, like a painter filling in a canvas.

He was doing the same with Kay, slowly, calmly filling in her personality, bit by bit.

In a while, when he had the strength, he'd get up and glance in at the kitchenette, even into the refrigerator she'd just mentioned, since he was curious about what little things might have been left there.

There were photographs scattered around the apartment, probably Jessie's, among them one of a very dignified old woman who was probably her mother.

He'd ask Kay all about it. She could talk without worrying he'd be bored.

'Drink.'

And she drank, after he did, from the same glass.

'You see, François, that it's not so glittery after all. You were wrong.'

Wrong about what? The words were too vague. But he understood.

'You see, now that I've known you . . .'

Softly, so softly that he had to make out the words, she said, 'Move over a little, will you?'

And she slid down beside him. She was almost naked and he was fully clothed, but she didn't mind – it was no less intimate.

Her lips at his ear, she whispered, 'You know, nothing has ever happened here. I swear it.'

He was without passion and without desire. He would have had to go a long way back, perhaps to his boyhood, to recapture a sensation as sweet and pure as the one he experienced now.

He was caressing her, and it wasn't her flesh he was caressing, it was all of her, a Kay he felt he was gradually absorbing into him even as he was being absorbed into her.

They stayed like that, lying together, eyes half closed, motionless, for a long time. They seemed to melt together, looking into the pupils of each other's eyes, and reading there a bliss they wouldn't forget.

For the first time, too, he wasn't worried about any consequences. Her pupils grew wide, her lips parted slightly, he felt her breath on his mouth, and he heard her voice say, 'Thank you.'

Their bodies disentangled. This time there was no fear that passion would be followed by recrimination. They could lie next to each other without shame or regret.

They moved in slow motion in sunlight so golden that it seemed to shine just for them, their bodies full of a marvelous heaviness.

'Where are you going, François?'

'To look in the refrigerator.'

'Are you hungry?'

'No.'

For half an hour or more he had been promising himself he'd look around the kitchenette. It was neat and freshly painted. In the refrigerator there was a slice of cold meat, some grapefruit, lemons, several overripe tomatoes, and a stick of butter in wax paper.

He ate the slice of meat with his fingers, like a boy chewing on an apple he'd stolen from an orchard.

He was still chewing when he joined Kay in the bathroom, and she said, 'You see? You were hungry.'

He shook his head stubbornly, grinning and chewing.

'No,' he said. Then he burst out laughing. She didn't understand.

7

Two days later he went to the radio studio for the broadcast; he was playing a Frenchman again, a pretty ridiculous role. Hourvitch didn't shake his hand. He looked very much the important director, sleeves rolled up, red hair on end, his secretary running after him, notebook in hand.

'What do you want me to say, old man? At least get a telephone. Leave your number with my people. Unbelievable that there are still people in New York without a phone.'

It didn't matter. He'd kept calm, serene. He'd left Kay for the first time in – how many days? Seven? Eight? But the number was meaningless because it felt like forever.

He had wanted to bring her to the studio, hoping she'd wait for him in the anteroom.

'No, darling, you should go, *now*.'

He remembered that *now*, which had made them laugh and meant so much to both of them.

And yet here he was betraying her again – or so it seemed to him: from Sixty-sixth Street he should have taken the bus to Sixth Avenue. Instead, though night was falling, he decided to walk.

He had promised, 'I'll be home at six.'

'Don't worry about it, François. Come back whenever you want.'

Why had he repeated, needlessly, 'Six at the latest'?

At six, or close to it, he walked into the bar at the Ritz. He knew what he was hoping to find, and he wasn't proud of it. Every evening around this time Laugier was there, most often with other Frenchmen or foreigners living in New York or else passing through.

The atmosphere at the Ritz was a little like Fouquet's, and when he had first arrived in the United States, and didn't yet know where he was going to stay or how he was going to make a living, reporters had shown up there to take his picture.

Did he know why he'd come that day? Perhaps from some need to betray her, to make room for all the bad things fermenting inside him to freely expand in, because he wanted to get back at Kay – more than anything, that was why.

But get back at her for what? For all the days and nights they'd spent together alone, in a solitude that he wanted to be still more absolute, more intense, so much so that he'd even gone shopping with her over the last few days, had helped her set the table, had assisted her with her bath . . . He had done everything, done it of his own free will, hunting for anything that might serve to create a total intimacy between the two of them, obliterating every last remaining trace of shame or self-consciousness, even the kind that soldiers living in barracks continue to feel.

He wanted her more than anything. So why, when she was waiting for him, when he had told her to wait – why was he going to the Ritz instead of catching a bus or taking a taxi?

'Hello, old man!'

He wasn't looking for casual company, which he'd always hated. Perhaps he wanted to prove to himself that the leash wasn't too short, that he was still free and, in spite of everything, still François Combe?

There were four of them there, maybe six or eight, around two low tables. There was a lot of superficial friendliness, so it was hard to tell who had known each other for ages and who was there for the first time, who was paying for the latest round, or how, leaving, anybody found his hat in the teetering pile on the coat rack.

'May I introduce . . .'

An American girl, pretty, with lipstick on her cigarette and the looks of a model.

Introductions were going around, and he heard, from time to time, 'One of our greatest French actors, I'm sure you know his name, François Combe.'

Some rat-faced Frenchman, an industrialist or speculator – Combe didn't know why he disliked him so much at first sight – was staring his way.

'I had the pleasure of meeting your wife a few weeks ago . . . Wait. It was at a party at the Lido. I happen to have in my pocket . . .'

A French newspaper that had just reached New York. Combe hadn't bought a French newspaper in months. There was a photograph of his wife on the front page: 'Marie Clairois, the charming and talented star of . . .'

Combe wasn't upset. Laugier, who didn't understand, cast him a glance to calm down. No, he wasn't upset at all. And this was the proof: after everyone had left, many drinks later, when he was alone with Laugier, he brought up Kay.

'I want you to do me a favor. I want you to find a job for a girl I know.'

'How old is "this girl you know"?'

'I'm not sure. Thirty, maybe thirty-three.'

'In New York, old man, that's no longer what you'd call a girl.'

'Which means?'

'She's played out. Sorry for putting it so crudely, but I think I've got the picture. Is she good-looking?'

'That depends what you mean by good-looking.'

'The old story. She started out as a showgirl fourteen or fifteen years ago, right? Yes, she grabbed the brass ring and then dropped it.'

Scowling, Combe fell silent. Maybe Laugier was feeling sorry for him, but Laugier couldn't see the world except through his own eyes.

'What can this charming maiden of yours do?'

'Nothing.'

'Now don't get all worked up, dear boy. I'm saying this for your own good, and for hers, too. Here, in this country, you know, there's no time for games. I'm asking you, seriously, what can she do?'

'Seriously, nothing.'

'Could she be a secretary, a receptionist, a model? Anything?'

Combe had been wrong. It was his fault. He was already paying the price of betrayal.

'Listen, old man . . . Waiter, another round!'

'Not for me.'

'Shut up! Listen, I'm going to tell it to you straight. Understand? I saw you come in just now, and you looked like hell. It was the same thing last time I saw you with Hourvitch. And you don't think I have a clue, do you? Your girl says she's thirty, thirty-three. In the real world, that means thirty-five. You want some good advice, even though you won't take it? Well, here it is: leave her. And since we're on the subject, let me ask: Do you have some sort of understanding with this girl?'

He was furious at himself, furious at being made to feel small in front of Laugier, who wasn't half the man he was. He answered stupidly, 'None.'

'So what's the big deal? There's no brother, no husband, no lover to blackmail you, is there? You didn't kidnap her, did you? There aren't any charges against you like the kind they worry a fellow to death with over here? You didn't transport her across state lines to sleep with her, did you? I hope not – then you'd really be in trouble.'

Why didn't he just get up and go? What was wrong with him? Was it the manhattans? If their love hung in the balance because of a few drinks . . .

'Can't you be serious for once?'

'I am serious, old man. Okay, I'm joking, but it's when I'm joking that I'm most serious. This thirty-three-year-old girl of yours has no profession, no job, no money in the bank – let's face it, she's nothing. Do you understand? I don't have to take you to the Waldorf to prove my point. We're in a bar for men. But just step through the door, go down the hall, and you'll see fifty girls, each prettier than the last, all between eighteen and twenty, some of them even virgins, and every single one of them in exactly the same position as your thirty-three-year-old. And yet in a few hours forty-eight of them will go home, God knows where, wearing a thousand dollars' worth of jewelry, after having stopped for a ketchup sandwich at a cafeteria on the way. Did you come here to work, or what?'

'I don't know.'

'Well, if you don't know, go back to France and sign the first contract they offer you at the Port-Saint-Martin or the Renaissance. I know you'll do what you like anyway, and that you'll never forgive me for saying it, but you're not the first friend I've seen come here and get into trouble. You want to keep going the way you're going? Fine. You want to play *Romeo and Juliet*? Fine. In that case, good night, old man. Waiter!'

'No, I'll –'

'I've yelled at you enough that I should pick up the tab. What has she told you, your girl? She's divorced, of course. At that age here, they've all been divorced at least once.'

Why, exactly, was Kay divorced?

'She's been around, hasn't she? Now she's looking for a little stability.'

'That's not it, not really.'

And he surrendered all self-respect, because he didn't have the strength to betray her any further.

'Can you swim?'

'Sort of.'

'Sort of. Good. In other words, if you fell in you could get out, if the water wasn't rough or too cold. But if you had to save yourself along with someone hanging on to you for dear life, could you do it? Come on, tell me.' He waved at the waiter for another round. 'Well, old boy, she'll hang on, believe me. And you'll both sink like stones. The day before yesterday, when you left, I didn't say anything, because you weren't able to talk sense. Today you seem more rational.'

Combe, repentant, bit his lip.

'When I saw you stick your coin in the slot, you see . . . And wait for the record to start like a lovesick girl . . . No, old man, not you, not us. We know this business and how it works. At least let me tell you, since I'm an old friend and a good one: François, you're lost.'

Combe's change came. He drained his glass, counted out the tip, and stood up.

'Where are you headed?'

'Home.'

'God! Home, where you don't even have a phone – or do you expect producers to come track you down?'

They went out onto Madison Avenue, where the doorman stood waiting to summon a taxi.

'Look, brother, at home you only get one chance to roll the dice. Here you get two or three chances. But don't push it. I can show you girls who started out in a chorus line or behind a typewriter at sixteen, who were riding around in a Rolls-Royce at eighteen, and were back in the theater again at twenty-two, starting all over again. I've known some who hit the jackpot two, three times, then had to go back to business after having a Park Avenue penthouse and a yacht in Florida, but who still managed to get married again. Did your girl keep her jewelry, at least?'

Combe wasn't about to reply. What was there to say?

'From my limited experience, the thing to do would be to get her a job as an usherette in a cinema. Or even better! With the right connections . . . You hate me right now, don't you? That's a pity. Or maybe not. Everybody hates the doctor who operates on them. You deserve a lot better, old man, and when you realize it, you'll be cured. Bye-bye.'

Combe must have had too much to drink. He hadn't noticed because of how quickly one round had followed another in the noisy bar, and because of the anxious wait to talk to Laugier, which he'd allowed to go on far too long.

He remembered his wife's photo on the front page of the Paris newspaper, the fluffy hair around her head, which was a little too large for her shoulders.

The film people always said that was what made her look so young, that and her not having any hips to speak of.

Was Laugier some kind of clairvoyant? Maybe he really knew what was what. 'Usherette in a cinema,' he'd said. 'Or even better!'

Better, for sure. Because she wasn't healthy enough to be an usherette.

'Here you get two or three chances.'

Then, as he was walking alone in the shining light of the window displays, he experienced a revelation.

Kay had been gambling, she'd been gambling and he was her final throw of the dice. Yes, he had come along at the very last minute. Fifteen minutes more, or if something else had grabbed his attention as he turned into the diner – if, for example, he'd chosen a different stool – then maybe one of the drunk sailors . . . or someone else . . .

But he'd had enough of his cowardice. She was very dear to him. He had to hurry home to reassure her. He wanted to tell her that no matter how condescending they acted, all the Laugiers on earth could never destroy the tenderness they felt for each other.

He was a little drunk, he realized. He'd bumped into a passerby and then elaborately doffed his hat to apologize.

But he was sincere. All the rest of them, all the Laugiers – like that rat-faced Frenchman who'd had a couple of drinks and then made off triumphantly with the young American girl – all of them, all of those people at the Ritz, at Fouquet's, they were all asswipes.

And the word, which he'd just hauled up from the depths of his memory, pleased him so much he had to say it again, out loud: 'A bunch of asswipes.'

He couldn't stop.

'Asswipes, that's what they are. I'll show them . . .'

Show them what? He didn't know. It didn't matter.

He'd show them . . .

He didn't need Laugier or Hourvitch – Hourvitch, who wouldn't shake his hand and who barely seemed to recognize him – he didn't need anyone!

'Asswipes!'

His wife, too. She'd never had to roll the dice two or three times, she'd won the prize on the first throw, and she wasn't even content. And now she was using everything she'd gotten from him in order to further the career of a gigolo!

Because it was true. When he'd first brought her onto the stage, she'd been nothing, playing bit parts, awkwardly opening a door and stammering, 'Dinner is served, Countess.'

And she became Marie Clairois. He'd even made up her name. Her real name was Thérèse Bourcicault, and her father sold shoes in the market in a little town in the Jura. He remembered the night he'd explained the name to her, at a restaurant called La Crémaillère, on the avenue de Clichy, over a red-checkered tablecloth and boiled lobster.

'Marie, you see, is so French. Not only French, but universal. Because it's so ordinary, no one except a housemaid would be called Marie anymore, so it's become original again. Marie . . .'

She had asked him to repeat it.

'Marie . . . And now, Clairois. There's "clear" in it . . . And "clarion," sort of . . . There's –'

Good God! What was he thinking? He didn't give a damn about Marie Clairois or her gigolo, whose only claim to fame was going to bed with his wife.

And Laugier, that self-satisfied, condescending idiot, talking about his 'girl of thirty-three,' about the jewelry she didn't have, about getting her a nice little job – if she had connections!

A few weeks earlier, before Kay, Laugier had asked him, with the monumental conceit of a man who thinks he's God Himself, 'How long can you hold out, dear boy?'

'Depends what you mean.'

'Enough to have your suits dry-cleaned, your laundry done, enough money in your pocket to pick up a bar bill or hop into a taxi.'

'I don't know. Five months, maybe six. When my son was born, I set up a trust fund that matures when he's eighteen, but I suppose I could dip into that.'

Laugier couldn't give a damn about Combe's son.

'Five or six months, good! Find a place to live, any-where, in a slum if you have to, but at the very least get yourself a telephone.'

Hadn't Hourvitch told him the same thing today? But he wasn't going to be bothered by that. He really should have taken the bus, though there weren't a lot at this hour. But what difference would a few minutes more or less make to Kay, who'd be waiting up anyway?

Kay!

How different the name sounded now from the way it had two, three hours before, or that morning, or at noon, when they were sitting across from each other over lunch smiling at the tailor across the street, to whom Kay had had delivered, anonymously, a truly magnificent lobster.

They were so happy! No matter how Kay's name was sounded, it filled him with peace.

He'd given the taxi driver his address. The sky above the streets looked black and menacing. He leaned back sullenly against the seat. He hated Laugier. He hated the rat-faced man. He hated everybody. He was wondering if maybe he hated Kay, too, when the taxi came to a sudden stop, and before he'd had time to pull himself together, to be her lover again, he saw her outside, on the sidewalk, haggard and out of breath.

'François! Oh, at last! Come quick! Michelle . . .'

Then she began frantically speaking in German.

The atmosphere in the room was close and heavy. Each time he came back in from the street, it seemed even darker, though all the lights were on.

He had been up and down the stairs three times; it was nearly midnight. His coat was drenched, and his face was wet and cold. The rain had started to pour violently.

The question of the phone would not leave him alone; it had hounded him all day long. Kay couldn't be blamed for the state of her nerves right now, but she had snapped, 'Why on earth don't you have a phone?'

Another coincidence: Enrico had come with the telegram in the late afternoon at almost the exact moment when Combe was sneaking guiltily into the bar at the Ritz. If only he'd come home when he'd promised . . .

Not that he was jealous. Though maybe Kay had cried on Enrico's shoulder, and probably he had tried to console her.

And another coincidence: the day before, while they were shopping for dinner, Kay had said, 'Maybe I should give the post office my new address. Not that I get much mail, but . . .'

Because she was still trying hard not to make him feel jealous, she'd added, 'I should have given Enrico the address, too, in case anything's showed up at Jessie's.'

'Why don't you call him?'

He had no idea, at that moment, how important his words would turn out to be. They went into the drugstore, as they had before. Through the glass he watched her lips moving but couldn't tell what she was saying.

He hadn't been jealous.

That day, Enrico had gone to Jessie's place for his things. He'd found some mail for her and Kay. There was a telegram for Kay that had come the day before.

It came from Mexico, so he brought it to her. She was alone in the room, making dinner. She had on the pale blue nightdress that made her look like a newlywed.

MICHELLE SERIOUSLY ILL MEXICO CITY
STOP BANK OF COMMERCE AND INDUSTRY
AUTHORIZED TO ADVANCE YOU TRAVEL
EXPENSES IF NECESSARY STOP

LARSKI

Larski wasn't telling her what to do. He left her free to decide. But he had foreseen that she might be short of money, and, in his chilly way, he had made the necessary arrangements.

'I didn't even know he'd brought her to America. Her last letter came four months ago.'

'Whose letter?'

'My daughter's. She doesn't write very often. I suspect she's been forbidden to and has to do it on the sly, though she doesn't admit it. Her last letter came from Hungary, and she said nothing about a trip. What could be the matter with her? Her lungs are fine. We've had her examined by the best specialists since she was a baby. Do you think she might have had an accident, François?'

Why had he had all those drinks? Just now, trying to console her, he'd been embarrassed about his breath – sure that she would notice he'd been drinking. He felt weighed down. He was unhappy.

It was as though something oppressive had settled on his shoulders even before he came home. He couldn't shake it off.

'Eat, François. You can call later.'

No. He wasn't hungry. He went downstairs to use the telephone at the Italian place.

'It won't work, you'll see. There's no overnight flight to Mexico. Enrico already tried.'

If he'd come home on time, Enrico wouldn't have stuck his nose in something that didn't concern him.

'There are two flights tomorrow morning, but all the seats are taken. It seems you have to reserve them three weeks in advance.'

He called even so, as if the miracle might come through for him.

He went back upstairs empty-handed.

'The first train's at 7.32 in the morning.'

'I'll take it.'

'I'll try to get you a sleeper.'

And again he went down to call. Everything was gray and dreary. He came and went dejectedly, like a ghost.

On the phone, they transferred him from desk to desk. He wasn't used to American railroad companies.

The rain, coming down hard, spattered the sidewalk and filled the brim of his hat. When he tipped his head, it spilled to the floor.

Why did these ridiculous details bother him so much?

'It's too late to make reservations. The man told me to be at the station half an hour before the train leaves. There's always somebody who doesn't show up.'

'I'm putting you to so much trouble, François.'

He looked at her carefully, not knowing why, and the thought struck him that it wasn't because of her daughter that Kay sounded so miserable. She was thinking about them, about how in a few hours they'd be separated.

The telegram, that horrible scrap of yellowish paper, meant bad luck. It was the sequel to Laugier's words and to Combe's own thoughts that night.

There was no escape, now, from whatever fate held in store.

Most disturbingly, he was almost resigned to its verdict.

He sensed a weakness, a passivity in himself, a dull lack of response that disheartened him.

She was packing. She said, 'I don't know what to do about money. The banks were already closed when Enrico came. I could take a later train. There must be one.'

'Not till evening.'

'Enrico wanted to . . . Now, don't get angry! You know, nothing else matters right now! He said that if I needed money, I could call him at home, even at night. I didn't know if you –'

'Would four hundred dollars be enough?'

'Of course, François. Only . . .'

They still hadn't talked about money.

'It really isn't a problem.'

'Maybe I could give you a note or something, I don't know, that you could take to the bank tomorrow, and they'd give you the money instead.'

'It can wait until you get back.'

They didn't look at each other. They were too scared. They were saying the words, but they didn't really believe what they were saying.

'You should get some sleep, Kay.'

'I couldn't.'

'Go to bed.' It was the kind of pointless thing people say at such moments.

'Do you think it's even worth it? It's already two. We'll have to leave here at six, in case we don't find a taxi.'

She almost said – he thought she almost said – 'If only we had a phone . . .'

'That means we'll have to be up at five. You'll want a cup of coffee, won't you?'

She lay down on the bed, fully dressed. He paced around, then lay down beside her. Neither spoke or closed their eyes. They both stared at the ceiling.

He'd never felt so depressed, so filled with despair that was without an object, for which he had no words, and against which there was no defense.

He whispered, 'You'll come back?'

Without answering, she found his hand under the cover and squeezed it hard.

'I wish I could die instead of her.'

'Stop it. Nobody's going to die.'

He wondered if she was crying. He passed his hands over her eyes and they were dry.

'You'll be all alone, François. That's what hurts me the most. Tomorrow, when you come home from the station . . .' A sudden thought alarmed her, and she sat up, looking wide-eyed at him. 'You're taking me to the station, aren't you? You must! I'm sorry for asking, but I don't think I could go through with it alone. I know I have to go, and you have to make me go, even if –'

She buried her face in her pillow, and neither of them spoke, lost in their separate thoughts, preparing for the loneliness that lay ahead.

She slept a little. He dozed off for a very short while and then got up to make the coffee.

The sky was even darker at five in the morning than at midnight. The streetlights did nothing to dispel the gloom, and the spitting rain threatened to continue all day.

'Time to get up, Kay.'

'All right . . .'

He didn't kiss her. They hadn't kissed all night – perhaps because of Michelle, perhaps because they both were afraid of losing control.

'Dress warmly.'

'All I have is my fur.'

'Wear a wool dress, at least.'

They managed to say meaningless things like 'It's always hot on the train.'

She drank her coffee but couldn't eat anything. He helped her close her overstuffed suitcase, and she looked around the room.

'Do you mind if I leave the rest of my things here?'

'It's time to go. Come on.'

There were only two lit windows on the whole street. Other people who had a train to catch? People who were sick?

'Stay in the doorway. I'll go to the corner and try to find a cab.'

'We'll lose time.'

'If I don't find one right away, we'll take the subway. You'll stay here, won't you?'

Stupid question. Where was she going to go? He turned up his coat collar, lowered his head against the rain, and, keeping close to the buildings, ran for the corner. He'd just made it when he heard her voice behind him: 'François! François!'

Kay stood in the middle of the sidewalk, waving her arms. A taxi had stopped two doors away, bringing a couple home after a night out.

Some coming home, others heading out – it was like the changing of a guard. Kay held the cab door open and spoke to the driver while Combe fetched her suitcase from the doorway.

'Grand Central.'

The car seat was sticky with the humidity, everything was soaked all around, the air was raw. She pressed herself against him. They kept silent. No one was in the streets. They didn't even see another car until they reached the station.

'Don't get out, François. Go home.'

She had laid an emphasis on the last word, to give him courage.

'There's still an hour to wait.'

'It doesn't matter. I'll get something warm at the bar. I'll try to eat something.'

She forced a smile. The taxi had stopped, but they didn't get out, not yet ready to run through the curtain of rain that separated them from the building.

'Don't get out, François . . .'

It wasn't cowardice – he actually didn't have the strength to climb out, to follow her into the labyrinth of the station, to stare at the ticking hand of the huge clock, to live through their parting, minute by minute, second by second, following the crowd when the gates were opened, catching sight of the train.

She leaned over to him, and there were raindrops on her fur coat. Her lips were burning. They clung to each other for a long moment, the driver's back to them, and Combe saw the light in her eyes, heard her stammer, as in a dream, 'Somehow now it doesn't feel like going away . . . it feels like coming home.'

She pulled herself away from him. She had opened the door and gestured to a porter to take her suitcase. Combe would never forget the three quick steps she took, her momentary hesitation, the rain-streaked glass, the rain spattering on the sidewalk.

She turned, smiling, her face pale. She held her purse in one hand. One more step and she would disappear through the immense glass doors.

Then she waved with her other hand, without lifting it much, only reaching out to him slightly, letting her fingers say good-bye.

He saw her again, half hidden by the glass. Then she walked off behind the porter with quick, brisk steps, and the driver turned around to ask him where he wanted to go.

He must have told him the address. And without thinking, he had filled his pipe. His mouth felt furry and dry.

She had said, 'Like coming home . . .'

He sensed a promise of sorts there.

But he didn't understand.

8

My dear Kay,

Enrico has told you what happened. So you know
that Ronald has been very nice about it all, very much
the gentleman; he's acted throughout just the way
you'd expect him to, not even going into one of those
cold rages of his, which I don't know how I could have
handled, given the state I was in . . .

Combe hadn't taken a nosedive, which is what he'd
expected. Instead it had been like slowly sinking, day by
day, hour by hour.

For the first few days, at least, he was restless but
still normal enough. All through that endless night,
which now seemed so short, he had begged, 'You'll
call me?'

'Here?'

He'd sworn that he would have a phone installed
immediately. He'd set about getting one the very first
morning, afraid it would take too long and he'd miss
her call.

'Will you phone me?'

'Of course, darling. If I can.'

'You can always call if you really want to.'

'I will, I promise.'

The phone had been installed. It turned out to be so easy that he was almost annoyed he hadn't had to move heaven and earth to get it done.

The city was gray and grubby. It rained. Now sleet was falling, darkening the street to such an extent that it was hard to make out the Jewish tailor in his cell-like room.

The phone had been installed ever since the second day, and he hadn't dared to go out, even though Kay could barely have made it to Mexico.

'I'll call information in New York,' she'd explained. 'That's how I'll get your number.'

He'd already called information five or six times to make sure they knew he was connected.

How strange it was. Kay seemed to have melted away into the rain. He really did see her as through a rain-streaked window, a bit blurry, distorted, but that made him cling even harder to the image of her he was desperately trying to hold in his mind.

Letters came for her, forwarded from Jessie's address. Kay had told him, 'Open them all. There won't be any secrets in them.'

And yet he hesitated. He let them pile up. He didn't decide to look until, on one, he spotted the blue-and-orange logo of Grace Lines. It was a letter from Jessie airmailed from the Bahamas.

. . . the state I was in . . .

He knew them all by heart now.

. . . if I hadn't wanted to avoid a scene at all costs . . .

And it was all so far away. It was like looking through the wrong end of a telescope and seeing things taking place in a world that made no sense.

I know, if push had come to shove, Ric would have left his wife without a second thought . . .

He repeated it to himself: 'If push had come to shove!'

. . . but I chose to go away. It's going to be painful. And it will probably take a while. This is a tough time. How happy we were together, my poor Kay, in our little apartment!

I wonder if those days will ever return. I'm afraid to hope. Ronald gives me chills and he puzzles me, and yet there's nothing I can reproach him for. Instead of those terrible rages he used to go into, he's so calm now he scares me. He doesn't leave me alone for a minute. Sometimes I feel he's trying to read my mind.

And he's so sweet, so thoughtful. More than ever before. More than on our honeymoon. Do you remember the story I told you about the pineapple that made you laugh so hard? Well, that could never happen now.

Everybody on board thinks we're newlyweds, and sometimes it's just so funny. Yesterday we broke out our linens because we're coming into the tropics. It's already hot. It seemed strange to see everybody in white all of a sudden, even the officers. There's a young one (he has only one stripe) who keeps making eyes at me.

Don't say anything to poor Ric, who'd just get upset.

I don't know how things are with you back there, my poor Kay, but I imagine they must be pretty awful. When I put myself in your place, I can picture your confusion and only hope you're making out somehow . . .

It was a strange feeling. There were times when he felt almost relieved, his head clear, unclouded, moments when the world was free of shadow, looking so crisp and fresh that it was almost physically painful.

My dear Kay,

This letter had a French stamp and a Toulon postmark. Hadn't Kay told him to open them all?

I haven't heard from you in nearly five months now, but I'm not too surprised, since it's you . . .

He read slowly, because every word held a special meaning for him.

When we got back to France, there was a surprise waiting for me that at first I found pretty unpleasant. My submarine and a few others had been transferred from the Atlantic to the Mediterranean fleet. In other

words, my home port is now Toulon instead of good
old Brest.

It wasn't so bad for me, but my wife, who had just
rented a new house and got all settled in, was so disappointed that she fell ill . . .

This one, Combe knew, had slept with her. He knew
where and under what circumstances. He knew everything, down to the last detail, since he'd practically begged
to know. It hurt him and pleased him at the same time.

We're living now in La Seyne. It's a sort of a suburb,
not too nice, but the tram stops outside my door, and
there's a park across the street where the children can
play . . .

That's right, he had children, too.

Chubby is fine and getting fatter than ever. He sends
his regards.

Chubby!

Fernand is no longer with us. He was assigned to the
Naval Ministry in Paris. It's what he needed, city boy
that he is. He'll do well at the parties in rue Royale,
especially the big receptions.

As for your friend Riri, all I can say is that we
haven't spoken, except in the line of duty, since we left
the shores of wonderful America.

I don't know whether he's jealous of me or I of him.

He probably doesn't know either.

It's up to you, my little Kay, to settle the argument and . . .

He dug his fingernails into the curtain. And yet he was quite calm. He was still calm. It was only the first few days. He was so calm that he mistook the emptiness around him for real emptiness, and it was then that he thought coldly, *It's over.*

He was free again, free at six in the evening to have as many drinks as he wanted with Laugier, to talk with him as much as he liked.

If Laugier asked about that 'thirty-three-year-old girl,' he was free to say, 'Who?'

And there was no denying that it made him feel a little better. Laugier was right. It was bound to turn out badly. There was no way it could turn out well.

Sometimes he wanted to see Laugier again. On several occasions he got as far as the entrance to the Ritz, but he felt too guilty to go in.

Other mail came for Kay, mostly bills. Among them was one from the dry cleaners and there was another from a milliner who'd done something to a hat of hers, probably the one she'd worn on the night they met. He could see it now, perched over one eye, and right away it assumed the value of a memento for him.

Sixty-eight cents!

Not for the hat, but for doing something to it. To have a ribbon put on or taken off, some small, silly, feminine thing.

Sixty-eight cents . . .

He remembered the amount. And he remembered that the milliner was on Twenty-sixth Street. Then, in spite of himself, he imagined the way there, the way Kay, on foot, must have gone, as if during one of their long night rambles.

They'd done a lot of walking, that was for sure.

Nobody had called since the phone had been put in, nobody could have, since no one knew he had one.

Except Kay. Kay had promised, 'I'll call as soon as I can.'

But Kay hadn't called. He was afraid to go out. For hours he sat, hypnotized, watching the Jewish tailor. He now knew when he ate, when he assumed or abandoned his hieratic pose at his worktable. Combe lived across the street from this other loneliness, and he knew what it was like.

And he was almost ashamed of the lobster they'd had delivered. Because now he could imagine himself in the other man's place.

My little Kay . . .

Everybody called her Kay. It was enraging. Why had she told him to open her letters?

This one was in English, stilted, formal.

I received your letter of August 14. I was delighted to discover that you were in the country. I hope the Connecticut air is doing you good. Business matters have made it impossible for me to escape from New York for as long as I might have wished.

However . . .

However what? He'd slept with her, too. They all had! Would the nightmare ever end?

. . . my wife would be delighted if you . . .

Bastard! But no. Combe was the one who was wrong. And he didn't have to be. It was all over. All he had to do was write, 'Finished. Period, new page.'

Yes, a period and then a brand-new page – and he wouldn't have to suffer anymore.

That was what he was thinking. That he'd suffer to his dying day on account of her.

And he was resigned to it. Idiotically.

What would a fool like Laugier say about that?

But it was simple, so simple that . . . Well, what was there to say?

That's how it was. Kay wasn't there, and he needed Kay. He'd seen himself as a tragic figure once because his wife, at the age of forty, wanted to fall in love again, to feel young again. Could he have been any more childish? Did it even matter?

He knew now it didn't. The only thing that mattered, the only thing in the world that was important, was Kay, Kay and the life she'd led, Kay and . . .

. . . and a phone call. That was all, just one phone call. He waited day and night. He set the alarm for one in the morning, then two, then three, to be sure he'd be awake enough to hear the ring.

At the same time, he said to himself: *It's fine. Everything's fine. It's over. It couldn't have ended any other way.*

Because he could taste disaster on his lips.

No, really, it couldn't have ended any other way! He'd become François Combe again. They'd welcome him, at the Ritz, like a man recovering from a serious operation.

'Well, it's all over?'

'Yes.'

'It didn't hurt too much? You're not still sore?'

But there was no one at night to hear him pleading into his pillow, 'Kay! My little Kay . . . Please call, please!'

The streets were empty. New York was empty. Even their little bar was empty, and, one day when he wanted to play their song, he couldn't because a drunk they'd tried to throw out, a Scandinavian sailor – Norwegian or Danish – had grabbed him by the elbow and insisted on divulging his incomprehensible secrets.

Wasn't it better like this? She was gone for good. She knew it, they both did. For good.

'Now it doesn't feel like going away . . . it feels like coming home.'

What had she meant? Why like coming home? Home where?

Dear Madam: You have probably overlooked our bill for . . .

Three dollars and change for a blouse he remembered having taken from Jessie's dresser and put in the trunk.

That was Kay – a threat to his peace of mind and to his future, Kay who was Kay, who he could no longer do without.

He would forsake her ten times a day and then just as many times or more he'd plead for forgiveness, only to forsake her again minutes later. And he avoided men as if they were dangerous. He hadn't gone to the radio studio once. He hadn't seen Hourvitch or Laugier. He hated them now.

Finally, on the seventh day, or rather the seventh night, while he was fast asleep, the telephone shattered the silence of his apartment.

His watch lay beside it. It was two o'clock.

'Hello.'

He could hear the long-distance operators exchanging messages. One insistent voice repeated stupidly, 'Hello . . . Mr Combe . . .? Hello, Mr Combe . . .? C . . O . . . M . . . B . . . E? Hello . . . Mr Combe . . .?'

In the background he could hear Kay's voice, but she hadn't been connected yet.

'Yes . . . This is Combe. Hello?'

'Mr François Combe?'

'Yes, yes.'

And she was there, at the other end of the night. She asked softly, 'It's you?'

And he found nothing better to answer with than 'It's you?'

★

He had told her once, at the start – and she had laughed – that she had two voices: one that was banal, that could have been anyone's, any woman's; the other was deeper, lower. He had loved that one from the very first moment he heard it.

He had never heard her voice over the telephone before, and happily it turned out to be the deeper one, a little lower-pitched even than he remembered, warmer, with a hint of a drawl, tender and seductive.

He wanted to shout, 'It's over, Kay. I'm not going to struggle anymore.'

He understood. He would never abandon her again. He was impatient to tell her, since he had only figured it out just now.

'I couldn't call any sooner,' she was saying. 'I'll explain everything later. It's all good news down here. Only it's been very hard to call. It still is. But from now on I'm going to try every night.'

'Can't I call you? You're not at the hotel?'

Why was there a pause? Did she guess that he already felt betrayed?

'No, François. I had to move into the embassy. Don't worry. And especially don't think anything's changed. When I got here, they'd just finished operating on Michelle. It seems to have been very serious. Acute appendicitis, and then peritonitis suddenly set in. Can you hear me?'

'Yes. Who's there with you?'

'The maid. A nice Mexican woman who has a room on the same floor. She heard some noise and wondered if I needed something.'

He heard her say a few words to the woman in Spanish.

'Are you still there? Anyway, my daughter. She's had the best surgeons in the country. The operation went well. But for several days there was a danger of complications. And that's that, my sweet.'

She had never called him that before, and it had a depressing effect on him.

'I think about you, you know, all alone in your room. Are you very unhappy?'

'I don't know. Yes . . . no.'

'Your voice sounds funny.'

'Really? It's because you've never heard me on the telephone. When are you coming back?'

'I don't know yet. As soon as I can, I promise. In three or four days, maybe.'

'That's a long time.'

'What did you say?'

'I said, that's a long time.'

She laughed. He was sure he heard her laugh.

'Imagine, I'm barefoot and in my bathrobe, since the telephone is by the fireplace and it's chilly tonight. And you? Are you in bed?'

He didn't know what to answer. He didn't know what to say anymore. He had looked forward to this, he'd been waiting so long for it that now he didn't know who she was.

'Have you been good, François?'

He said he had.

And then, at the other end of the line, he heard her humming, very softly, their song.

He felt something warm welling up in him. He couldn't move or breathe. He couldn't speak.

She finished the tune, and after an interval – was she crying, or was she, too, unable to speak? – she whispered, 'Good night, my François. Go to sleep. I'll call you tomorrow night. Good night.'

He heard the faint sound of the kiss she was sending him across all that space. He must have stammered something. The operators were back on the line, and he didn't understand that they were telling him to hang up.

'Good night.'

And that was that. And his bed was empty.

'Good night, *my* François.'

And he hadn't told her what he wanted to tell her, he hadn't cried out the all-important message, the good news she had to know.

Only after he'd hung up did the words form on his lips.

'You know, Kay . . .'

'What, sweetheart?'

'What you told me at the station. The last thing you said.'

'Yes, sweetheart . . .'

'That you weren't going away, that you were coming home.'

She would have been smiling. He could see that smile so perfectly that it was as if he were hallucinating it, and he spoke out loud, all alone, in the emptiness of his room: *'I understand, at last, what you meant . . . It's taken me a while, hasn't it? But don't be angry with me.'*

'No, sweetheart.'

'Because men, you know, aren't as subtle as women . . . And they're too proud . . .'

'Yes, sweetheart. It doesn't matter.'

In a voice so low, so soft . . .

'You came home first, but I'm with you now . . . We're both home now, aren't we? And isn't it wonderful?'

'It's wonderful, sweetheart.'

'Don't cry . . . You mustn't cry . . . I'm not crying, either. But I'm not used to it yet. Do you understand?'

'Yes.'

'It's over now . . . It's been a long time, and the going was sometimes hard . . . But I'm here . . . And I know . . . I love you, Kay . . . Can you hear me? I love you . . . I love you . . . I love you!'

And he buried his wet face in his pillow, his body racked with sobs, while Kay was still smiling at him, while her soft, deep voice was whispering in his ear: 'Yes, sweetheart.'

9

A letter came for him in the morning mail, and even without the Mexican stamp he would have known that it was from Kay. He'd never seen her handwriting before. But it was exactly like her! He was very moved by this Kay – girlish, hesitant, and so terribly imprudent, a Kay nobody else knew.

He was probably being ridiculous, but in the curves of certain letters he thought he recognized the curves of her body. Some of the down strokes were very fine, like the imperceptible lines on her face. And there were sudden, unexpected forays into boldness. And a lot that was weak as well; a graphologist might have detected her illness, because he was certain, almost convinced, that she was still ill, that she had never been fully cured, and would bear her sickness with her all her life.

And her cross-outs, so oddly candid, when she stumbled on some syllable she couldn't spell.

She hadn't mentioned the letter during last night's phone call, probably because there hadn't been time. Perhaps there was too much else she wanted to say, or she'd just forgotten.

It was not as gray as it had been, and though the rain still fell, now it seemed like background music to his thoughts.

My darling,

How alone and unhappy you must be! I've been here for three days now and I haven't had time to write or found a way to telephone. But I've never stopped thinking about my poor François, who must be having a bad time there in New York.

Because I'm sure you're feeling lost and alone, and I still wonder what I did, what you possibly see in me that makes my presence so necessary to you.

If only you could have seen how miserable you looked in the taxi at the station! It took all my courage not to turn around and come back to you. Can I tell you that it made me happy?

Perhaps I shouldn't say this, but since New York you've never been out of my thoughts, even when I'm with my daughter.

I'll telephone you tonight or tomorrow night, depending on how my daughter is doing. Since my arrival I've spent every night at the hospital, where they set up a bed for me in a room next to Michelle's. I admit I didn't dare ask for a line through to New York. Either I call from my room, where the door to my daughter's room is always open, or I call from the office, which is run by a dragon lady in eyeglasses who doesn't like me.

If all goes well, this will be my last night at the hospital.

But I'll tell you everything, because otherwise, I know, you'll imagine all sorts of things and just torture yourself.

First of all, I confess right away that I almost deceived you. Don't worry, my poor darling. You'll soon see what I mean. After I left you in the taxi and bought my ticket, all of a sudden I felt so alone that I raced to the restaurant. I wanted to burst into tears, my poor François! I could still see you looking out through the taxi window, all haggard and tragic.

There was a man next to me at the counter. I wouldn't recognize him if I saw him again or be able to say if he was young or old, but I said to him: 'Talk to me, will you, please? I have twenty minutes before my train leaves. Say anything at all, anything, so I won't burst into tears right here in public.'

I must have looked like an idiot, once again. I was certainly acting like one, I realized afterward. But I needed to talk, to pour out my heart to somebody, and I don't remember what I told that stranger for the next quarter hour.

I talked about you, about us. I told him I was going away and that you were staying behind.

Then I thought I still had time to call you. It was only when I was in the booth that I remembered you didn't have a phone yet.

I ended up on the train, I don't know how, and I slept all day. I didn't even have the strength to walk to the dining car. All I had to eat was an orange.

Is all this boring to you? My daughter is asleep. The nurse has just gone out; she has to look after another patient on the floor and has to change the ice bag on the patient's stomach every hour.

I'm in my little bed like the one at the sanatorium, in a whitewashed room with a little light shining on the stationery, which is propped up against my knees.

I think about you, about us. I still wonder how it's possible. I wondered about that during the whole trip. You see, I can't get rid of the feeling that I don't deserve you! And I'm afraid of hurting you again. You know what I mean, my François, but I'm convinced now that one day you'll realize that this is the first time I've been in love. Are you beginning to feel it yet? I hope you are for your own sake. I don't want you to be hurt anymore.

I must stop writing about these things, otherwise I might pick up the phone and call New York whether Michelle can hear or not.

I was surprised to find her already quite grown up. She looks like me, much more like me than she did when she was small, when everyone said she took after her father. She's noticed it, too, and she looks at me – I'm sorry if I seem just a little conceited writing this – she looks at me, as I said, with a sort of admiration.

When I got to the station after two days of traveling, it was already past eleven. On the off chance, I'd sent a telegram from the border, and a car from the embassy was waiting for me at the station.

It seemed funny to be alone in a limousine crossing through a brightly lit city where the people were only just waking up. The driver said, 'Madame needn't worry. The doctors believe the young lady is out of danger. The operation yesterday was successful.'

I was glad that Larski didn't meet me at the station. He wasn't at the embassy, either, where I was met by a sort of governess, very Hungarian and very much the great-lady-who-has-fallen-upon-hard-times. She showed me to the apartment set aside for me.

'If you wish to go to the hospital tonight, a car from the embassy is at your disposal.'

I don't know if you understand how it felt, sweetheart, to be all alone in that huge place with nothing but my poor suitcase.

'The maid will run a bath for you. Afterward, you will no doubt wish to eat something?'

I don't remember if I did eat. They rolled a table, all set, into my room like in a hotel. There was a bottle of Tokay, and I have to confess, and you can either laugh at me or scold me, that I drank it all.

The hospital was on a hill at the edge of town . . . Everything was very formal. Larski was in the waiting room with one of the surgeons who had just examined Michelle. He bowed to me. By way of introduction, he said: 'The mother of my daughter.'

He was in formal dress, which isn't that odd since he'd obviously just come from some diplomatic function, but it made him look icier than ever.

The doctor said that in his opinion the danger was over, but that he wanted another few days to be sure. It was only when he went away and Larski and I were left alone in that sort of sitting room that reminded me of a convent, that Larski, who was as cool and poised as ever, gave me the details.

'I hope you were not annoyed by my slight delay in notifying you, but I had some trouble locating your current address.'

And you know, sweetheart, that it wasn't my current address, because we were at our place!

Forgive me for those last two words, but I have to write them, to say them out loud, to convince myself that it's true. I was unhappy – I know you must have been, too – and I should have been with you, which I know so well is the place where I belong.

In the middle of the night they decided to operate. I'm trying to tell you everything, but my thoughts get a little mixed up. Do you realize I still don't know how long Michelle has been in Mexico? We've barely had a chance to talk, and anyway she's so shy around me that she hardly says a word. If I start talking, the nurse signals me to be quiet. It's even written on the walls!

What was I saying, François? I forget how many days, exactly, I've been here. I sleep in the nurse's room, but she's hardly ever there, as I think I've already told you, because she has to spend so much time with the other patient, who's also a young girl.

Michelle often talks softly in her sleep. She speaks in Hungarian and mentions names I don't know.

In the morning, I help bathe her. She has a little body that reminds me of mine when I was her age, and it brings tears to my eyes. She's as shy as I was then. For one part of the washing-up she won't let me stay in the room, even if I turn my back.

I don't know what she thinks of me, or what people have told her about me. When she looks at me, she's both curious and astonished. When her father comes, she looks at us without saying anything.

I think of you all the time, François, even – and I know this is not a nice thing to write – even the other evening, at about ten o'clock, when Michelle fell unconscious and everyone was so scared that they telephoned the opera to have her father paged.

Am I a heartless monster?

Larski looks at me strangely. Sometimes I wonder if something hasn't changed in me since I met you, since I fell in love with you, if there isn't something new in me that even people who don't care about me notice.

Even the Hungarian lady at the embassy – you should see the way she looks at me!

Because every morning a car comes to take me back from the hospital. I go straight up to my apartment. I have my meals there. I've never laid eyes on the dining room, and what I know of the rest of the place comes from a glimpse I once caught passing through, when they were doing the cleaning and all the doors were open.

The only real conversation I've had with Larski was in his office. He telephoned me one day to ask if I could meet him there at eleven.

Like everyone else, he looked at me with some surprise. There may have been a hint of pity in his expression, too; probably because of my dress, my hands without rings on them, and my face, since I haven't bothered to put on makeup. But there was something more than pity in his eyes. I don't know what it was and can't explain it. It's as if people can sort of sniff out love, and it sets them on edge.

He asked me, 'Are you happy?'

I said yes, very simply and looking him straight in the eyes, and he blinked first.

'I am taking advantage, if that is the phrase, of the occasion that has accidentally thrown us together again to inform you of my forthcoming marriage.'

'I thought you were already remarried.'

'I was. It was a mistake.'

He made an elegant gesture with his hand. Don't be jealous, François, but he really has very beautiful hands.

'I am remarrying, beginning my life again, and that's why I brought Michelle here, because she will have a place in my new home.'

He thought I was going to burst into tears or turn pale, I don't know. And the whole time, I swear it, I beg you to believe me, I was thinking about you. I wanted so much to say to him, 'I'm in love!' But he already knew it. He could tell. It's impossible for people not to tell.

'That, Katherine, is why . . .'

Again I'm sorry, I don't want to hurt you, but I have to tell you everything.

'That is why you must not be angry about being excluded from the daily life of this house, and why I hope your stay here will not be unduly prolonged. I have tried to do my duty.'

'I thank you for it.'

'There are several other matters that I have wanted settled for some time, and, if I have not done so, it is only because I had been unable to locate you.'

I'll tell you all about it when I see you, François. I haven't made any hard-and-fast commitments. But please believe that everything I've done was for your sake, with you in mind, and in the belief that we will always be together.

Now you know pretty much everything about my time here. Don't on any account think I'm being humiliated. I'm a stranger in this house, and I speak to no one except the Hungarian lady and the servants. They're polite and distant. Except for one of the maids, a girl from Budapest, whose name is Nouchi. One morning she surprised me getting out of my bath and said, 'Madame has skin exactly like Miss Michelle's.'

You, too, my love, told me one night that you liked my skin. My daughter's is much softer and whiter. Her skin . . .

But here I am, getting sad again. I didn't want to be sad tonight when I wrote to you. But I wanted so much to send you something worthwhile!

And I have nothing to give you. On the contrary. You know what I'm thinking, what you're thinking all the time, in spite of yourself, and it frightens me, until I wonder if I should return to New York at all.

If I were a real heroine, like the ones people talk about, I probably wouldn't come back. I'd disappear, as they say, without a forwarding address, and perhaps you'd soon find someone to console you.

I'm not a heroine, my François. As you can see! I'm
not even a mother. At my daughter's bedside, it's my
lover I'm thinking about, my lover I'm writing to, and
I'm proud to write that word for the first time in my life.

My lover . . .

Like in our song – do you still remember it? Have
you gone out to listen to it? I hope not – imagining
your poor head hearing it, I'm scared you might drink
too much.

You mustn't. I wonder what you do with all the days,
your long days of waiting. You must spend hours and
hours in our room, and by now I'm sure you know every
detail in the life of our little tailor, who I miss, too.

I don't want to think about it anymore, or else I'll
call you and risk making a scandal. That is, if you did
manage to get a phone installed so quickly!

I don't know yet if it'll be tomorrow night or the night
after that Michelle will be well enough for me to sleep at
the embassy, where there's a phone in my bedroom.

I've already asked Larski in passing, 'Would you
mind if I made a call to New York?'

I could see his jaw tighten. Now don't start imagining things, my love. It's an old tic of his. It's about the
only sign of emotion anyone can make out on his face.

And I think he would have been quite happy to find
that I was alone in the world, even desperate!

Not to take advantage of it, you idiot! That's all
over. But because he's so incredibly proud.

He replied coolly, bowing from the waist, another
tic of his that helps a diplomat, 'Whenever you wish.'

He knew. And I, my love, wanted to shout your name in his face: 'François!'

If this goes on much longer, I'll have to talk to somebody about you, anyone, the way I did at the station. You won't hold that stupid story at the station against me, will you? You know, don't you, that it was all because of you, because I couldn't carry you around with me all by myself for so long?

I remember how you looked when you said, 'You just can't help turning on the charm, can you, even for a cafeteria boy or a taxi driver? You're so desperate for attention from men that you demand it from the beggars you give a dime to in the street.'

Well, I'm going to confess something else. No, I'd better not; you wouldn't understand. But so what? What if I said that I almost told my daughter about you, that I did mention you to her, vaguely – oh, very vaguely, so don't worry – as if I were talking about an old friend, someone I can always trust . . .

It's already four o'clock in the morning. I had no idea. I've run out of paper. I've already written in all the margins, as you can see, and I wonder what kind of sense you are going to make of it all.

I want so much for you not to be sad, for you not to be lonely, for you to have confidence in us, too. I'd give anything not to see you hurt because of me.

I'll call you tomorrow night or the night after. I'll hear your voice, you'll be at our place.

I'm just worn out.

Good night, François.

That day, he experienced such deep happiness that he knew no one could see him and not notice it.

It was so simple. It was simply beautiful!

He still had some nagging worries, like the pangs of a convalescent, but he was entirely enveloped by an immense serenity.

She would come back. Life would begin again.

That was all.

And all he had to do was think: *She'll come back, she'll come back. Life will begin again.*

He didn't want to laugh, to smile, to dance, but he was happy, calm, dignified. And he didn't want to start worrying.

The fears were obviously ridiculous, right?

The letter was written three days ago . . . In three days who knows what could happen?

He used to try to imagine the apartment Kay shared with Jessie, before he'd actually seen it, and of course he'd been entirely wrong. Now he imagined the vast embassy in Mexico City, with Larski, whom he'd never seen, sitting in his office in front of Kay.

What had he proposed to her that she'd accepted without accepting, that she wouldn't tell him about until later?

Would she call again tonight? At what time?

Because she didn't know. He'd been silent on the telephone. She knew nothing of what had been going on inside him. She still didn't know he was in love with her.

How could she know, since he himself hadn't known until a few hours ago!

So, what would happen next? Would they still be in tune with each other? He wanted to tell her the news, to explain everything right now.

Since her daughter was out of danger, why didn't she come home? Why was she wasting time down there anyhow, surrounded by all those dreary, hostile presences?

And her idea of disappearing without a trace, just because she'd hurt him and would hurt him again!

No, no! He had to explain . . .

Everything was different now. She had to know. Otherwise she might do something stupid.

He was happy, he was awash in happiness, tomorrow's happiness, the happiness of a few days later, but which he felt, for now, almost as anguish, since it wasn't in his grip yet, and he was terrified it would slip away.

A plane crash, for instance. He'd have to ask her not to fly home. But then he'd be waiting another forty-eight hours or more . . . Are there that many more plane crashes than train wrecks?

He'd talk to her about it, at least. He could go out, since she'd told him she wouldn't call until tonight.

Laugier had been an idiot. That wasn't the right word. He'd been perfidious. Because the way he had talked the other evening had been nothing short of perfidious. Because he, too, must have sensed what Kay had described, that aura of love that enrages people who aren't in love.

'In a pinch we might get her a job as an usherette . . .'

Not his exact words, but that was what he'd said about Kay!

Combe didn't have a drink all day. He didn't want to drink. He stayed calm, savoring his tranquility – because in spite of everything, it was tranquility.

Only at six in the evening did he decide to go see Laugier at the Ritz – though now he felt he'd known all along that he was going to do it – not so much to confront him as to show him just how tranquil he was.

Things might have turned out differently if Laugier had laughed at him, as he'd expected him to, or just been a trifle less aggressive.

There was a crowd at the bar, including the young American girl from the time before.

'How are things, old boy?'

Just a quick look. Self-satisfied, the handshake slightly warmer than usual, as if to say: 'See? All over and done with. What did I tell you?'

Did the idiot think it was finished, that he'd left Kay?

And that was that – no use talking about it. The whole thing was over and done with. Combe was once more a man like any other.

Did they really believe that?

Well, Combe didn't want to be a man like any other. They were just pitiful – that was what he needed to feel. He missed Kay so much that a wave of dizziness swept over him.

It was impossible that they hadn't noticed. Or was he really normal, like these people that he despised?

He acted normally, accepted first one and then a second manhattan, and talked to the American girl, who was getting lipstick all over the tip of a cigarette and asking him about his work onstage in Paris.

He longed desperately, almost painfully, for Kay to be there, and yet he behaved like any other man, surprising himself by showing off, talking about his theatrical successes with more animation than he should have.

The rat-faced man wasn't there. There were other people he didn't know who claimed to have seen his films.

He wanted to talk about Kay. He had her letter in his pocket and, at times, he would have pulled it out and read it to whoever would listen – that American girl, for instance, though he had hardly noticed her the week before.

They don't know, he said to himself. *They couldn't know.*

Obediently he drank the cocktails that were set down before him. He thought: *Three more days, four at most. She'll call me again tonight, and she'll sing our song.*

He was in love with Kay, no doubt about it. He'd never loved her more than he did that night. And that very night he was going to discover a new dimension to their love, perhaps its very essence.

But everything was still confused and would stay confused, like a bad dream.

The self-satisfied smile on Laugier's lips, for instance, the ironic light in his eyes. Why was Laugier making fun of him now? Because he was talking to the American girl?

Fine, he'd talk to her about Kay. He no longer knew how it had happened, how their conversation had strayed onto this particular topic.

Ah, yes! She'd asked him, 'You're married, aren't you? Is your wife here with you in New York?'

And he spoke about Kay. He told her that he had come to New York alone, and loneliness had made him understand the priceless value of human contact.

That was the phrase he'd used, and at this moment it seemed to him so charged with meaning that, in the heat of the Ritz, in the middle of the noisy crowd, with a glass before him that he kept draining, it was like a revelation.

He'd been alone and terribly unhappy. And he'd met Kay. And immediately they'd experienced the most intense intimacy imaginable.

Because they'd been so starved for human contact.

'You don't understand, do you? You couldn't understand.'

And then the smile from Laugier, who was at the next table, chatting with a producer.

Combe was sincere, passionate. He was full to overflowing with Kay. He remembered the first time they had fallen into each other's arms, knowing nothing about each other except that they were both starved for human contact.

He repeated the phrase, tried to find its equivalent in English. The American girl watched him with eyes that grew thoughtful.

'In three days, maybe sooner if she takes a plane, she'll be here.'

'How happy she must be.'

He wanted to talk about her. Time was passing too quickly. The bar was emptying, and Laugier stood, holding out his hand.

'I'm off, kids. By the way, François, will you be good enough to see June home?'

Combe had a vague feeling he was the object of a conspiracy, but he wouldn't believe it.

Hadn't Kay given him everything a woman possibly could?

Two wandering creatures, set apart on the surface of the globe, lost in the thousand identical streets of a city like New York.

And fate brings them together. And just a few hours later, they were so tightly bound to each other that the idea of ever being apart again is intolerable to them.

Wasn't it a miracle?

It was that miracle he was trying to explain to June, who looked at him with eyes in which he read a yearning for the worlds he was opening up for her.

'Which way are you going?'

'I don't know. I'm not in any hurry.'

So he took her to his little bar. He needed to go there, but he didn't have the strength, that night, to go alone.

June wore a fur, too, and she, too, took his arm just like that.

It was a little like having Kay there. Hadn't they talked about Kay and nothing else?

'Is she pretty?'

'No.'

'Really?'

'She's very exciting. She's beautiful. You'd have to see her. She's *the* woman, you see? No, you don't understand.

A woman who's seen a lot of life but has stayed a child. Let's go in here. I want you to hear . . .'

He fumbled in his pocket for nickels and played the song, looking at June and hoping that she'd feel everything that it had meant to *them*.

'Two manhattans, please.'

He knew he shouldn't go on drinking, but it was too late to stop. He was so moved by the music that tears came to his eyes, and June stroked his hand as if to comfort him.

'You shouldn't cry. She's coming back.'

He clenched his fists.

'But don't you understand that I can't wait anymore, that two days, three days is an eternity?'

'Hush! People are looking at you.'

'I'm sorry.'

He was too wound up. He didn't want to relax. He played the record once, twice, three times, then again, and each time he ordered more cocktails.

'At night we'd walk up and down Fifth Avenue for hours.'

He was tempted to do the same with June, just to show her, so she could share all his anxieties and fears.

'I'd love to meet Kay,' she said, staring into space.

'You'll meet her. I'll introduce you.' He meant it. He said it without regret. 'There are so many places in New York now where I can't bear to go to alone.'

'I understand.'

She took his hand again. And she looked moved, too.

'Let's go,' she said.

Go where? He didn't want to go to bed alone in his room. He had no idea what time it was.

'I know! I'll take you to a nightclub where Kay and I used to go.'

And in the taxi, she nestled against him, slipping her bare hand into his.

Then it seemed to him – no, it was too hard for him to find the right words. It seemed to him Kay wasn't just Kay, but everybody in the world, all the love in the world.

June didn't understand. Her head was on his shoulder, and he breathed in a perfume he didn't recognize.

'Promise me you'll let me introduce her to you.'

'Of course.'

They walked into the Number One bar, where the pianist was still trailing his fingers over the keyboard. She walked ahead like Kay, with the same instinctive pride of a woman carrying a man in tow. She sat down, and, like Kay, shrugged her fur off her shoulders, opened her purse, found a cigarette, searched for her lighter.

Was she, too, going to speak to the maître d'?

It was late, and there were traces of fatigue under her eyes – like Kay. Her cheeks had begun to sag under her makeup.

'Do you have a light? My lighter's out.'

She blew out the match and laughed smoke into his face. A moment later, she leaned over and brushed his neck with her lips.

'Tell me more about Kay.'

But suddenly she grew impatient. She stood up and said, 'Let's go.'

Once again, where? Except that now they both sensed the answer. They were in Greenwich Village, not far from Washington Square. She was clinging to his arm, leaning against him as they walked, and he could feel her thigh pressing against his at every step.

And she was Kay. In spite of everything, it was Kay he was seeking, it was Kay he was touching, it was even Kay he heard when she spoke to him in a low voice, a little thick.

They stopped at his door. For an instant he stood motionless. He closed his eyes for a second. Then, with a gentle gesture, as if resigned to the inevitable, but also with a kind of pity for him, for her, and even more for Kay, he pushed her to go through the door.

She climbed the stairs a few steps ahead of him. There was a run in her stocking, too.

'Farther up?'

Of course she didn't know! She stopped on the next-to-last stair, averting her eyes.

He opened the door and reached for the switch.

'No. Please don't turn on the light.'

The room was faintly illuminated by the pale, too-focused light of street lamps that is the essence of night in the city.

He felt the fur, the silk dress, the warm body, and at last, the two moist lips seeking to mold themselves to his.

Kay . . . he thought.

Then they went under.

They lay without speaking or moving, body against body. Neither slept, and they both knew the other was awake. Combe's eyes were open, and beside him he saw the vague shape of a cheek and a nose that were a little shiny with sweat.

They knew they had to go on waiting in silence. Then there was a sudden explosion of noise – the telephone ringing so loudly that they both jumped, not even realizing what had happened.

Combe panicked, fumbling idiotically in the dark for the instrument he'd answered only once before. June switched on the bedside lamp.

'Hello . . . yes.'

He didn't recognize his own voice. He stood naked and stupid in the middle of the room, holding the receiver in his hand.

'François Combe, yes . . .'

June got out of bed and whispered, 'Where do you want me to go?'

Go where? She could hear just as well from the bathroom.

She lay back down on her side in the bed. Her hair fanning over the pillow was the same color as Kay's.

'Hello.'

His throat was tight.

'Is that you, François?'

'Of course, my love.'

'What's the matter?'

'Nothing. Why?'

'I don't know. Your voice sounds funny.'

'I just woke up.'

He was ashamed of lying – not just of lying to Kay, but of lying to her in the presence of this other woman who was watching him from the bed.

June had offered to leave the room – couldn't she at least show some tact and turn around? She was watching him out of one eye, and he couldn't help staring back.

'I have good news, darling. I'm leaving tomorrow, or rather this morning, by plane. I'll be in New York tonight . . . Hello?'

'Yes.'

'That's all you have to say? What's wrong, François? You're hiding something from me. You've been out with Laugier, haven't you?'

'Yes.'

'I'll bet you were drinking.'

'Yes.'

'I was sure that was it, my poor darling. Why didn't you say so? I'll see you tomorrow. Tonight.'

'Yes.'

'The embassy got me a seat on the plane. I don't know exactly when the flight's due in, but you can find out. I'm flying Pan American. Make sure you've got that, since two airlines fly the same route and the planes don't get in at the same time.'

'Yes.'

There were so many things he wanted to tell her! He had such wonderful news to tell her, and there he was, hypnotized by this watching eye!

'Did you get my letter?'

'This morning.'

'There weren't too many spelling mistakes? Did you read it through to the end? I don't think I'll go to bed tonight. It's not that it will take so long to pack. You know, I got out for an hour this afternoon and bought you a present. But I can tell you're sleepy. Did you really have that much to drink?'

'I think so.'

'Was Laugier very unpleasant?'

'I don't remember, darling. I was thinking about you the whole time.'

He couldn't go on. He was in a hurry to hang up.

'See you tonight, François.'

'Yes, tonight.'

He had wanted to tell her. He tried, as hard as he could, but he'd failed.

He should have said, straight out: 'Listen, Kay, there's somebody in the room. Now you know why I . . .'

He'd tell her when she got back. He didn't want to cheat on her. He wasn't going to allow anything so cheap to come between them.

'Go right back to sleep.'

'Good night, Kay.'

He put the phone down slowly. For a long moment he stood in the middle of the room, his arms at his sides, staring at the floor.

'Did she guess?'

'I don't know.'

'Will you tell her?'

He raised his head and looked her in the eyes. 'Yes,' he said calmly.

She lay for a moment on her back, her breasts showing, then she straightened her hair, lifted her legs out of bed, and began pulling on her stockings.

He didn't try to stop her. He wasn't going to ask her to stay. He started dressing, too.

She said, without bitterness, 'I'll go alone. You don't have to see me home.'

'I'll come with you.'

'You'd better not. She might call again.'

'You think?'

'If she suspects something, she will.'

'Please forgive me.'

'What for?'

'Nothing. For letting you go alone like this.'

'It's my fault.'

She smiled at him. When she was ready, and had lit a cigarette, she came over to him and kissed him lightly on the forehead. Her fingers sought his and squeezed them as she whispered, 'Good luck.'

Afterward he sat down in a chair, half dressed, and waited the rest of the night.

Kay didn't call. The first sign of the new day was the light going on in the Jewish tailor's shop.

Had Combe been wrong? Was it always going to be like this – as he struggled to discover new depths of love?

His face didn't move at all. He was so tired, weary in body and spirit. He didn't seem to be thinking anything.

But he was sure – completely sure – that it was only tonight that he had truly and totally begun to love Kay. At least tonight was when at last he knew it.

That was why, when dawn dimmed the light from his bedside table, he was ashamed of what had happened.

IO

She wouldn't understand. She couldn't understand. It was impossible for her to know, for instance, that for the whole hour he'd been waiting at La Guardia airport he'd been wondering, without any romantic exaggeration, but just because he knew what state his nerves were in, if he'd be able to withstand the shock.

Everything he'd done that day, everything he was right now, would be so radically new to her that, in a way, he'd have to train her all over again to know who he was. And the agonizing question was whether their feelings would still be in tune. Would she be able to follow him as far as he had gone?

That was why, since morning, he'd done none of the things he had promised himself for days he would do before she returned. He hadn't even bothered to change the pillowcase where June's head had lain – hadn't even checked to see if she'd left lipstick stains on it.

What was the point? He was beyond all that! It was all in the past!

And he hadn't ordered in from the Italian place. He had no idea what there was to eat or drink in the refrigerator.

What had he actually done that day? She'd be hard-pressed to guess. It was still raining, sometimes lightly, sometimes heavily, and he'd dragged a chair to the window, opened the drapes, and sat down. The sky was dull, cruel, the light pitiless, painful to look at.

It was what he needed. Stained by eight continuous days of rain, the brick walls of the houses across the street had turned a sickly color. There was something heartbreakingly dreary about their curtained windows.

Was he actually looking at them? Later, he was astonished to he realize he hadn't paid attention even for a moment to their talismanic little tailor.

He was very tired. The thought of going to bed for a few hours crossed his mind, but he stayed where he was, his collar open, his legs stretched out, smoking pipe after pipe and tapping the ashes out on the floor.

He didn't move until, around noon, he abruptly got up, went to the phone, and, for the first time, called long-distance and gave the operator a number in Hollywood.

'Hello . . . That you, Ulstein?'

Ulstein wasn't a friend. He did have friends in Hollywood, directors, French actors and actresses, but he didn't feel like calling them today.

'This is Combe . . . Yes, François Combe . . . What? No, I'm calling from New York . . . Yes, I know that if you had something for me you would've written or cabled me . . . That's not why I'm calling . . . Hello? Operator, please keep the line open . . .'

Ulstein was an awful man he'd met in Paris, not at Fouquet's, but on the sidewalk outside, where you'd see him walking around just to make people think he'd been inside.

'Do you remember our last conversation out there? You told me that if I was willing to play smaller parts or, not to beat around the bush, minor parts, you'd be able to find me work . . . What?'

Combe smiled bitterly, since he could tell Ulstein was about to start talking big.

'Give me numbers, Ulstein . . . I'm not talking about my career. How much a week? . . . Yes, for any part at all . . . Damn it, that's none of your business! Just answer my question!'

The unmade bed to the one side, the gray rectangle of the window to the other. Raw white and cold gray. His voice was insistent.

'How much? Six hundred dollars? . . . In a good week? . . . Fine, five hundred. Are you positive? You're prepared to sign, say, a six-month contract at that rate? . . . No, I can't give you an answer now. Tomorrow, probably . . . No, no. I'll call you.'

Kay didn't know about that. Maybe she expected to come back to an apartment filled with flowers; she didn't know that he'd considered it and shrugged the idea off in disgust.

Was he right to wonder if they'd still feel the same way?

He was going too fast. He knew that he'd traveled, in almost no time at all, a long, steep path that men can take years to complete, often their whole lives, if they reach the end at all.

He heard church bells when he left the house; he started walking, his hands in the pockets of his beige trench coat.

And Kay couldn't know that it was now eight at night and he'd been walking since noon, except for the fifteen minutes it took to eat a hot dog at a lunch counter. He hadn't eaten at their diner. Why bother?

He walked across Greenwich Village toward the docks and the Brooklyn Bridge, and for the first time crossed the immense structure on foot.

It was cold and drizzling. The sky hung low with heavy gray clouds. The East River was covered with angry white crests of waves, the tugs sounded shrill whistles, and ugly flat-bottomed brown ferryboats carried passengers back and forth on unchanging routes, like trams.

Would she believe him if he told her he had walked all the way to the airport, stopping at most a couple of times in a bar along the way, the shoulders of his trench coat soaked, his hands in his pocket, his hat dripping wet, like someone in a mystery story?

He hadn't played the jukebox. He didn't need to.

And everything he'd seen on his pilgrimage through this gray world, the little dark men bustling about under electric lamps, the stores, the movie theaters with their garlands of light, the butcher shops, the bakeries with their disgusting pastries, the coin-operated machines that played music or let you knock metal balls into little holes, everything the whole great city could invent to help a lonely man kill time, he could look at all that now without revulsion or panic.

She would be there. She was going to be there.

That one last worry, which he dragged past block after block of buildings, brick cubes with iron staircases outside in case of fire, where the question was not how people had the strength to go on living there – that was easy enough – but how they had the strength to die there.

Trams went by, filled with ghastly, secretive faces. And children, little dark figures in the grayness on the way home from school, strained, too, for happiness.

Everything in the shops depressed him. The wood-and-wax mannequins in their hallucinatory poses, holding out their too-pink hands in pathetic beckoning gestures.

Kay didn't know about any of this. She didn't know anything. Not that he'd walked around for exactly an hour and a half in the airport, among other people who were also waiting, some huddled and anxious, others happy or indifferent or self-satisfied, not that he'd wondered if at the last minute he'd be able to hold out.

He kept thinking about the moment when he would see her again. He wondered if she'd be the same, if she would look anything like the Kay he loved.

The whole thing was even subtler than that, even deeper. He'd sworn to himself that the moment he laid eyes on her, he'd say, 'It's all over, Kay.'

He knew she wouldn't understand. It was almost a play on words. What was over was the walking, the chasing and hounding each other. The running after each other, the turning away and turning back – that was over.

He'd made up his mind, which was why his trip here had been so purposeful and so painful.

Because despite everything there was still the possibility that she wouldn't be able to follow him, that she wasn't at his level yet. And he couldn't wait.

It was over. That summed it up. He felt as though he'd run the whole cycle, looped the loop, fulfilled his destiny, or at least that fate had caught him.

In the all-night diner, when they were still total strangers, everything had already been decided.

Instead of asking why, instead of groping in the dark, resisting and rebelling, he said, with humility and without shame, 'I accept.'

He accepted everything. All their love and whatever was going to happen. Kay as she was, had been, and would be.

Could she really have understood that when she saw him waiting there, with so many others, behind the gray barrier of the airport?

She rushed toward him, trembling. She kissed him, unaware that he wasn't interested in kisses. She exclaimed, 'At last, François!' Then, like a woman, 'You're soaking wet.'

She wondered why he was staring at her so hard, looking like a sleepwalker, why he was dragging her through the crowd, pushing through almost savagely.

She almost asked, 'Aren't you glad I'm back?' Then she remembered her suitcase. 'We'll have to wait for my luggage, François.'

'I'll have it delivered.'

'But I might need some of my things.'

'Too bad,' he said. He gave their address at the ticket window.

'It would have been easy by taxi. I brought you something from Mexico, you know.'

'Come on.'

'Of course, François.'

In her eyes he glimpsed fear, also submission.

'Anywhere around Washington Square,' he told the driver.

'But . . .'

He didn't ask her if she was tired or if she'd eaten. He didn't notice she was wearing a new dress under her coat.

She took his hand, but he didn't respond. Instead he acted stiff, which took her aback.

'François?'

'What?'

'You haven't really kissed me yet.'

Because he couldn't kiss her here and now – that wouldn't mean anything. He did try, but it struck her as grudging. She was afraid.

'Listen, François.'

'Yes.'

'Last night . . .'

He waited. He knew what she was going to say.

'I almost called you a second time. Forgive me if I'm wrong. But the whole time I had a feeling someone else was there.'

They didn't look at each other. It reminded him of the other taxi, that earlier night.

'Answer me. I won't be angry. Although – in *our* room . . .'

He said, almost dryly, 'Someone was there.'

'I knew it. That's why I didn't dare call back. François . . .'

No! He didn't want a scene. He was so far beyond that! And her hand gripping his, her sniffling, the tears she was holding back.

He was impatient to be home. It was like a dream, the long road that has to be traveled, the end almost in reach, but always one last hill that remains to climb.

Would he have the will to do it?

Shut her up. Someone should tell her to shut up. He couldn't. She'd come back, and she thought that was enough. But he had moved on while she had been away.

She stammered, 'Did you really, François?'

'Yes.'

He said it coldly because he resented her for not being able to wait for the wonderful moment he had prepared.

'I didn't think I'd ever feel jealous again. I know very well I have no right to be . . .'

He saw the bright lights of the diner where they'd met and told the driver to stop.

She couldn't have expected anything like this. He knew she was crushed, choking back tears, but that's how it was. He said to her again, 'Come on.'

She followed submissively, uneasily, tortured by the mystery he'd become. He said, 'We'll have something to eat and then go home.'

And like a character in a mystery with his wet trench coat, his soaking hat, and his pipe, he stepped out of the taxi into the light. For the first time he had lit his pipe while they were in a taxi.

Without asking what she wanted, he ordered her bacon and eggs. He ordered her brand of cigarettes and offered her one before she could look in her purse.

Was she beginning to guess what he hadn't yet been able to say?

'What I can't understand, François, is why it had to be the night when I was so happy because I knew that I'd be coming home.'

She could see him looking at her, more distantly than he ever had, even on the night they'd first met, just in this spot.

'Why'd you do it?'

'I don't know. Because of you.'

'What do you mean?'

'Nothing. It's too complicated.'

He was glum, removed. She needed to talk. 'I have to tell you – unless it bothers you – what Larski did. I haven't accepted anything yet. I wanted to talk to you first.'

He already knew. Anyone looking at them that night would have thought that he was heartless. But that was unimportant, nothing compared to the decision he'd made, to the truth that had finally dawned upon him.

She was going through her purse wildly. It was in bad taste, but she was so frantic he didn't hold it against her.

'Look.'

She held up a check for five thousand dollars.

'I want you to understand exactly . . .'

Of course. He understood.

'He didn't do this in the spirit you think. I have a right to it, according to the terms of our divorce. But I never wanted to bring up the question of money, just as I didn't demand to see my daughter so many weeks a year.'

'Eat.'

'Am I annoying you?'

'No.' The reply was sincere.

Had he foreseen this? Almost. He was too far ahead. He was going to have to wait, like the first person to make it up a hill.

'Waiter. The salt, please.'

Here she was, starting all over again. The salt. The pepper. The Worcestershire sauce. A light for her cigarette. Then . . . He wasn't impatient. Instead of smiling, he maintained the formal, grave demeanor he'd displayed at the airport. That was what unnerved her.

'If you knew him, especially if you knew his family, you wouldn't be surprised.'

Surprised? By what?

'For centuries they've owned huge, huge estates. There were times when they made a lot of money. I don't know if they still do, but they're colossally rich. But they've kept up certain customs. I remember, for instance, one crazy old man, some kind of eccentric or a con artist, I don't know which, who'd been living in one of their castles for ten years, supposedly cataloging the library. He read all day long. From time to time he jotted down notes on little scraps of paper and threw them into a box. After ten years, the box caught fire. I'm sure he set it on fire himself.

'In the same castle there were three ancient wet-nurses.
I don't know whose wet-nurses, since Larski's an only
child, but they lived pretty well. I could tell you a lot more
stories like that.

'What's the matter, darling?'

'Nothing.'

He'd caught sight of her in the mirror, as on their first
night, looking a little blurry and distorted. Here was his
final test. He hesitated.

'Should I cash the check?'

'We'll see.'

'For me, it's . . . I mean, don't get angry, but I want to
pull at least some of my own weight . . . You understand,
right?'

'Of course, my love.'

He wanted to laugh. It was almost grotesque. Her poor
love was so far behind his. She couldn't conceive of his
love even though he was about to offer it to her!

And she was so scared and bewildered! She went back
to eating, doing it with deliberate slowness, trying to
stave off the unknown that lay ahead. She lit her inevitable cigarette.

'My poor Kay!'

'What? Why poor?'

'Because I've hurt you, a little bit, without meaning to.
But I think it was necessary. I didn't do it on purpose, but
simply because I'm a man. It might happen again.'

'In our room?'

'No.'

She looked grateful. She still didn't know. She hadn't realized that their room was almost a thing of the past.

'Come on.'

She fell in step beside him. June had known how to do that, too, their thighs touching as they walked.

'You know, you've really hurt me. I'm not angry with you, but –'

He kissed her under a streetlight – the first time ever that he'd kissed her out of pity. The moment hadn't yet come.

'Do you want to go to our little bar for a drink?'

'No.'

'What about the Number One bar? It's not far.'

'No.'

'All right.'

She followed along, obediently, without feeling too reassured. They came to their house.

'I never thought you'd bring her here.'

'I had to.'

He wanted to get it over with quickly. He pushed her into the stairway, almost the way he'd pushed June the night before, though he knew there was no real comparison. He saw the fur floating up the stairs in front of him, the pale legs that halted on the landing.

Then, he opened the door and turned on the light, and there was nothing but the empty room, cold and messy to greet her. He knew she wanted to cry. Perhaps he even wanted her to cry. He took off his trench coat, his hat, and his gloves. He took off her hat and coat.

Her lower lip was starting to tremble when he said, 'You see, Kay, I've come to a decision.'

She was still afraid. She was looking at him with a little girl's wide eyes, and he wanted to laugh. It was an odd state of mind to be in while saying what he was going to say.

'I love you. I know it now. No matter what happens, whether I'm happy or unhappy, I accept it. That's what I wanted to tell you, Kay. That's what I swore to myself I'd shout on the phone, not just the first night, but last night as well, in spite of everything. I love you, whatever comes, whatever I have to go through, whatever I –'

But now it was his turn to be perplexed. He had expected her to fall into his arms, but she remained in the center of the room, looking drained and distant.

Had he been right to worry about their not feeling the same way anymore?

He called out, as if she were a long way off: 'Kay!'

She didn't look at him. She remained aloof.

'Kay!'

She didn't come. Her first impulse wasn't to come to him. On the contrary, she turned her back. Then she ran into the bathroom, shutting the door.

'Kay . . .'

He stood, dumbfounded, in the middle of the room he had deliberately left in a mess, with his hands empty and his love out of reach.

II

He sat silently and without moving, in the depths of his chair, his eyes fixed on the door. There was no sound from inside. Time passed, and he calmed down, while his impatience melted into a gentle, suggestive mood, something like confidence, and he began to feel at ease.

Much later, without a noise, the door opened. He saw the knob turn, the door open, and she was there.

They looked at each other. She had changed, but he couldn't tell how. Her face or something about her hair was different. She wasn't wearing makeup and her skin was fresh. She'd been traveling all day but it didn't show.

She smiled as she came toward him, shyly, almost awkwardly, and it struck him as sacrilegious for him to be here witnessing the birth of this happiness.

Standing in front of his chair, she held out her hands to help him up. It was a solemn occasion – it was important that they should both be standing.

They didn't kiss. They held each other, cheek to cheek, saying nothing for a long time. The stillness trembled around them, until at last she let out in an undertone, 'You came back.'

Then he was ashamed to have foreseen the truth.

'I didn't think you'd come back, François. I didn't even dare hope you would. Sometimes I hoped you wouldn't.

Do you remember in the taxi at the station, I said to you at the time that I didn't think you'd ever understand?

'That it wasn't going away, but more like coming home . . . For me. And now . . .'

He felt her go limp in his arms. But he was weak and clumsy, too, faced with the wonderful thing that was happening to them.

He was afraid she would falter. He wanted to lead her over to the bed, but she protested feebly, 'No . . .'

It wasn't their place, that night. Squeezed together in the big threadbare chair, each could feel the other's pulse and the other breathing.

'Don't speak, François. Tomorrow . . .'

Because the sun would rise tomorrow and they'd enter a new life together forever.

Tomorrow they would no longer be alone. They would never be alone again. She shivered, and at almost the same time he sensed an old, nearly forgotten worry rise in his throat. Both had understood that even though they didn't want to, they had to look back at the loneliness they were leaving behind.

And they wondered how they'd survived.

'Tomorrow . . .' she said again.

They would no longer have or even need a room in Manhattan. They could go wherever they wanted, whenever. There was no need to listen to a record in a little bar.

The lightbulb hanging from its cord went on in the tailor's shop across the way, and she smiled, at once tender and teasing.

He squeezed her hand to ask her why, not needing words now.

She stroked his forehead and said, 'You thought you'd gone further than I had, didn't you? You thought you were far, far ahead of me, and all the while it was you, poor darling, who was behind.'

Tomorrow would be a new day. Now it was dawn, and far off, you could hear the city coming to life.

Why hurry? The day was theirs, and the days that would follow. The city no longer frightened them, not this one and not any other.

In a few hours, this room would vanish. There would be luggage in the middle of the floor. The chair they were in would become just another shabby piece of furniture.

They could look back without fear. Even the trace of June's head on the pillow had lost its horror.

The future was for Kay to decide. If she wanted, they could go back to France together, and with her at his side he'd pick up where he'd left off. Or they could go to Hollywood and start from scratch.

It was all the same to him. Weren't they starting from scratch anyway?

'Now I understand why you couldn't wait for me,' she said.

He wanted to hold her in his arms. He tried to, but she slipped away. In the early-morning light he saw her kneeling on the rug before him, kissing his hands, whispering, 'Thank you.'

They could get up, pull the curtains on the cold gray day outside, and look around at the room, so poor and naked.

It was a new day. Calmly, without fear or suspicion, and only a little awkwardly, because it was all so new, they began to live again.

They stood in front of each other, a few feet apart, smiling, in the middle of the room.

He said, as if this was the only way to translate all the happiness inside him, 'Good morning, Kay.'

And her lips shook as she replied, 'Good morning, François.' And after a long silence: 'Good-bye, little tailor. . .'

They locked the door behind them when they left.